THE MECHANIC

REINA TORRES

BROTHERHOOD PROTECTORS

ORIGINAL SERIES BY ELLE JAMES

To the women out there like me, looking for a man who loves whole-heartedly.

ACKNOWLEDGMENTS

Mahalo and Lots of Love to Elle James -
You opened up your world to other authors and I hope I've
done justice to your world!

THE MECHANIC - STORY SUMMARY

Adam Masterson had always been at home with any kind of work involving his hands. Joining the military had given him a chance to work on all kinds of vehicles, but after twelve years he'd left to help his sister take care of her daughter. Hank Patterson had offered him a job with the Brotherhood Protectors, but he was just fine with his life the way it was.

Or so he thought.

Blake Lennox wasn't Hollywood's 'it' girl. She was the 'chubby bestie' who was always good for a laugh. Until the day she saw something that was as damning as it was criminal. When they realized she wasn't going to keep quiet, they were going to do it for her.

She barely made it to Eagle Rock, Montana and that's when she met a man who did the one thing no one else seemed to do. See her the way she saw him... desirable.

Hiding only works so long, but Adam wasn't going to let her face them alone. Not then. Not ever. He was going to take care of her and fix things... because he's the Mechanic.

CHAPTER 1

IN THE EARLY MORNING HOURS...

Blake Lennox had never been an easy sleeper. There was always something worrying her, thoughts rolling around inside of her skull that kept her awake to all hours or held her just shy of that lovely REM sleep that most people enjoyed.

And the last two days had only made her problems worse.

Tap. Tap. Tap.

Whatever it was knocking on her window better go away.

Tap. Tap. Tap.

She sat up, eyes wide and that's when she remembered.

She was in her car.

Alarmed she turned to look out the window and saw a flashlight pointed at her and a face half-shadowed beside it.

Her heart leapt up in her chest and she reached for something to protect herself. She grabbed the first thing she touched and lifted a plastic mini M&M container. Yeah, big help.

"Uh, ma'am?" The man outside turned his flashlight

around to shine light on his badge. "I'm an officer with the Utah Highway Patrol. Sorry to startle you."

Relief sagged her shoulders and she dropped the M&M container on the passenger seat with an out blown breath. "Goodness. I didn't know what to expect when I woke up. Is something wrong?"

"I was just trying to make sure you were okay. The fact that you're a woman traveling alone, well, my sister drives a lot so I just wanted to make sure you were okay."

She felt horrible keeping the window shut but while he may have shown her his badge, trust was not high on her list for strangers at the moment.

And due to her experience in the last few days, she wouldn't even trust most people she knew.

"I'm sorry if I worried you, officer. I was trying to make it to the next town, but I was just too tired to keep my eyes open." She sat up a little straighter in her seat. "Was there a problem with where I'm parked?"

"No, ma'am." He grinned and shook his head. "This is a rest stop. You're more than welcome to sleep here for the rest of the night. I just worry when I see women traveling alone."

"Well, thank you." She let out another breath and set her hand on her chest hoping to calm the racing beat of her heart. "That's very sweet of you."

He started to move away and paused, leaning back to look in the window.

She saw his curious look and wondered what had brought him back. "Do you need my license or-"

"You're Blake Lennox!"

There went her heart rate again, shooting up and pounding through her veins. "Oh, you recognize me?"

"Of course! My wife watches all of your movies with her friends, and my daughters still have their 'Sharpshooter Sally' backpacks from the *Frontier Friends* show." The officer tucked his flashlight into the crook of his arm and fumbled into his pockets. "I've got my notebook somewhere. Dang it." Taking a chance, Blake lowered her window and smiled at him.

"Do you have your phone?"

His eyes popped wide open. "Why, yes... I do!" Reaching into his back pocket he pulled out his phone and unlocked it.

"You want to be in the photo?"

He shook his head and stepped back to take her picture. She would have gotten out of the car, but that worked too. "They love you and they talk about being on TV like that Montana girl, but I want them to get a real education, you know?" He fumbled with the phone. "How do I do this again?"

Pasting a smile on her face she held out her hand for the phone. "I can do that."

"Oh, cool. Great. Thanks."

Focusing on the phone in her hands, Blake took a picture and edited the photo so they wouldn't see the horrible state of her hair and then using the pen function, she signed the photo at the bottom.

When she handed the phone back, she met the deputy's grateful gaze. "And I agree about school," she told him and noticed that his expression sobered a little, "I have a masters in Electrical Engineering from Cal Tech. You should look up Danica McKellar and Mayim Bialik to start with. We're not the only ones who have degrees."

The officer looked contrite. "I'm sorry, Miss Lennox, I didn't mean-"

She touched his arm and gave him a real smile. "It's natural to want the best for your children, that's good. Just don't forget to encourage the artistic interests they have. You might be surprised how academics and art go hand in hand."

He looked down at the photo on his camera and sighed

before looking back in through her window. "I didn't mean to... actually, I'm sorry for saying that. I don't know what came over me."

Well, she did. She'd heard it over and over from all kinds of people, assuming that she was as ditzy as some of her characters. "Please give your daughters a hug for me."

She reached up and grabbed her seatbelt, pulling across her body to sink it into the buckle.

"I should be getting on my way. Is there anything else-"

"Oh no. No. Sorry. Thank you again, Miss Lennox."

He backed away from the car and she thought for a quick moment that she should call him back and ask him to keep the meeting to himself. She probably shouldn't have allowed him to take the photo, but there was no getting that back now.

And she wasn't one to disappoint her fans. Especially the young ones who remembered her as 'Sharpshooter Sally.' As cheesy as the kids show had been, she still loved the messages that the kids took away from Sheriff Liberty and his Frontier Friends. So, she let him walk back to his patrol car before she pulled out of the space and headed for the on-ramp.

As for her interaction with the officer, she hadn't given him any real idea of where she was going, not that she had much of one herself. Her main focus was to put as much distance between herself and the troubles she'd left behind. And after his assumptions about her lack of an education, she hoped he might take a day or two before he even showed his girls the photo.

She could hope, couldn't she?

Testing her lights on the narrow exit lane from the rest stop she merged onto the road and continued on the highway, looking for an option.

~

ADAM MASTERSON WALKED into the diner to get a cup of coffee and maybe a pastry, but before he could find a table of his own, Hank Patterson flagged him over to the empty seat across from him.

In a town as small as Eagle Rock it would have been seen as more than a little rude to ignore him, even if he knew where this meeting was bound to go, so Adam walked over and set himself down in the empty chair.

"Morning, Hank."

Hank's smile summoned the waitress who greeted Adam with a smile and a cup of coffee filled up almost to the rim just like he liked it. "Good to see you, Annalise."

She gave him a cuff on the shoulder. "Good to see you too, brother."

Hank hid his laugh behind the lip of his cup.

Adam's sister gave him a pointed look. "You want me to put in an order for food? I can make it to go if you like."

Setting down his cup, Hank gave Annalise a side-look. "Trying to give him an escape route for this conversation?"

She held up her hands. An order pad in one, the other empty. "You're really good at this interrogation thing, aren't you? Just make sure you two play nice. People around here still think I'm a sweetheart, but if I have to drag you both out of here for fighting at the table, everyone's going to know I'm a smaller, stronger version of my brother."

"Well," Hank cleared his throat, "I don't want to blow your cover, Miss Masterson. Until then, I'll sit here nice and quiet." He gave Adam a pointed look. "I can't vouch for your brother, though."

Setting her hand on the back of Adam's chair, Annalise leaned down and pressed a kiss to his cheek. "Food?"

He shrugged and gave her a grudging smile when she told him she was ordering him a bowl of soup. "You're obsessed with feeding me."

Rolling her eyes, she took a step away. "You took care of me and Ada. Now it's my turn to worry over you a little, until we find you a wife." She turned a wide-eyed smile toward Hank. "You wouldn't have someone you could introduce my brother to, would you?"

Adam almost felt bad as Hank choked on thin air.

Almost.

"Leave the man alone, Annalise."

"I want to see you happy. So, sue me." She shrugged and moved away to put in Adam's order.

Hank looked across the table at him. "Looks like she's got her mother hen skills down."

"Tell me about it. Even when I was trying to care for her after Ada was born, I'd catch her trying to get up and make dinner. After a while I got her to stop by asking her if she didn't like my cooking."

Confusion settled over Hank's features. "Are you that bad of a cook?"

Adam sighed. "Why does everyone assume I'm crap in the kitchen?"

Hank wisely stayed silent.

"I'm a good cook. I won't say I'm better than Annalise, but I keep her and Ada happy when it's my night to cook. Still, it did get her to stop trying to be superwoman."

"Well, you're a good man, Adam. I don't doubt that. If I did-"

"The answer is still no." Adam took a sip of his coffee, wincing at the burning touch on his tongue. "Sorry if I jumped on that. I just," he struggled to find the words, "I just made my mom a promise that my focus was going to be on family. That's why I left the military when Annalise was put on bedrest during her pregnancy. If something happened to me when she needed me..." he let the words trail off because he didn't want to think about the alternatives.

"And then when Ada was born and the nurse put her in my hands-" Adam looked down toward the table and held his hands up in the same way he held his niece, remembering his first look at her precious face. A moment later, he busied his hands with the napkin sitting before him. "I knew where I was needed and what I was meant to do. Putting myself in the line of fire wasn't something I could do after that, and keep my conscience clean."

Annalise walked up and placed the soup cup and saucer before him, she gave them a look silently asking after their needs.

Adam waved her away with a wink and turned to look back at Hank.

The other man had lost the joking grin. "Why didn't you just say that before? I didn't know that was hanging over your head."

Picking up his spoon, Adam dipped it into his soup. "It's not something I wanted to say. I don't like to say things like that out loud much. My mom was the kind of woman who believed you should only say the good and positive things. If you give voice to the bad then it's like you're inviting it in."

Nodding slowly, Hank pondered his words. "I can see the reason in that, Adam. Now I see what you're dealing with. I'm sorry if I pushed too hard. I wasn't trying to make things harder. I just knew you from your record and what I knew... I needed."

Adam couldn't help but smile at the other man's words. He wasn't someone who sought out platitudes, but when a man like Hank tells you that you're good enough to make his 'must have' list, that's gold.

"Thank you," Adam let out a breath and felt his shoulders and the tense muscles along his neck relax. "It's good to know." Needing to shift the tone of their meeting, Adam asked a question as he lifted his spoon toward his mouth. "How are Sadie and the baby?"

The change in Hank was immediate.

Sitting up in his chair, he reached for his phone and turned it on, turning it around so that Adam could see the lock screen.

Adam shook his head with a smile. "You're a lucky man, Hank."

After a moment, Hank, turned the phone back around and lowered it closer to the tabletop, but the smile never left his face. It might have changed, ever so slightly, a little softer, almost sweeter.

It was almost hard to reconcile the man he saw now to the one who had marched himself into Adam's mechanic shop and offered him a job.

Adam set his spoon down on the saucer, his appetite gone. He wasn't jealous of Hank, but he saw the affection in his eyes and read the ease of his shoulders. Hank was a man satisfied with his life.

Who didn't want that?

∼

LATE AFTERNOON...

Be careful what you ask for.

The words were whispered into her head with the distinct sound of her third-grade teacher who never quite liked Blake, no matter how much her little self had tried to change it.

And now, here she was, driving a car that she'd bought from a little old lady who had called the antique 'her little dear.' The woman had let her test drive it and she had and it had worked just fine. After an exchange of most of Blake's emergency cash that she'd brought with her, she'd told herself that she'd be okay as long as she made it to Eagle Rock.

And she had.

She just made it past the sign naming the town and its population when 'the little dear' backfired and sent Blake lurching forward, gripping the steering wheel as it swerved a little bit.

Just great.

Just flipping great.

Taking in a deep breath she continued down the street. Part of the problem of trying to get off and stay off the grid was that you can't do a whole lot of research on a town this small from a map you buy at a gas station.

All it gave her in the way of information had literally been a map dot, but still, there had to be a gas station here. And a gas station meant information and hopefully a guy that would check out her car without making too many comments about 'women and cars.'

That she could do without.

She looked up at a sign for the Blue Moose Tavern and grinned. That would be a must see if she wasn't here trying to lay low, but maybe someday.

Yeah. Keep it positive. Someday.

Blake rolled on past and kept her eyes glued to the signs up ahead.

If only she'd taken Sadie up on any of her prior invitations for a visit, this wouldn't nearly be as scary as it was. And Blake had no problem admitting that she was scared.

Scared was something she liked to overcome. It gave her a boost of pride, but this time it felt like something cold across the back of her neck.

So much so that she lifted her eyes to look into the rearview mirror.

Empty.

Thank goodness... the road behind her was blissfully empty.

When she lowered her gaze back to the street outside of her windshield she almost jammed on the brakes in relief.

Masterson Mechanics

"Thank God."

With a quick flick of her turn light she coasted into the flattop beside the building. When she set the car in park it made the most horrible gasping sound and something under the hood dropped.

Like her heart into her stomach.

When she sat back in the driver's seat the car shuddered from tail to hood and Blake imagined it sagging into the pavement beneath her like a cartoon in the old Bugs Bunny show.

"Overacting much?"

With a sigh of her own, Blake yanked the keys from the ignition and dropped it into her purse. She opened her door and felt the cool Montana air brush against her cheeks. It was the first fresh breath she'd had in hours.

Grabbing her purse, she stepped out and locked the door behind her before she walked toward the open bay doors.

There was someone walking around inside. She heard soft steps and drawers opening and closing. She could almost see the sweet old man inside with just her imagination. He had worked here for years, raising a family with his work-roughened hands.

Maybe he even enjoyed spending his off hours playing with his grandchildren in his front yard. Or maybe his dogs.

By the time she stepped inside the bay she was ready to be regaled by hundreds of pictures of his extended family, but the man that stepped out from behind the raised hood of a truck looked nothing like the Wilford Brimley she had created in her head.

Nope.

Just her luck, the man dressed in clean *and pressed* overalls looked like he stepped out of one of the hot firefighter calendars.

Blake lifted her free hand before she could stop herself and patted her hair. Yep, she lost a whole bunch of brain cells after just one look at the man.

He stopped a few feet away and looked her over. Inwardly she cringed. She was way out of her element. Sandwiched in the tiny VW Bug for the better part of the day she knew she looked a mess. She probably had her clothes all wrinkled.

But the sad part was, he was just out of her league.

The man was hot.

Her character in 'Wedding Wars' would have given him the eye and asked him if he'd want to, 'look under my hood.'

But Blake, the chubby best friend, was stunned into silence when he pulled a cloth out of his pocket and wiped his hands.

Two words.

Forearm Porn.

Wait! Was that three words?

Fore arm porn?

No, two!

OMG. She was losing her mind!

Who could blame her? The way his forearms rippled with muscle was so...

Hot.

HAWT.

"Miss?"

Her cheeks flushed with heat and she swallowed to clear her throat. "Yeah, sorry. I was a little stupid there for a minute."

He narrowed his eyes at her and tilted his head.

And while she stood there humiliated, he looked her over, again.

Why did she have to look like she was running away from home when she meets the hottest guy she's ever seen?

Because, her mind explained, *you're you and this is just the universe's long middle finger extended in your direction.*

"You don't look little or stupid."

The words caught her attention and she snapped her eyes up toward his face. What she saw there wasn't what she expected. There was no laughter at her expense in his eyes. He wasn't mocking her.

"Miss?"

Blake shook herself. "Sorry, I- I'm just a little confused."

Instantly, his expression changed. He went from keen and curious to concerned. "Are you okay?" He shoved the cloth back into his pocket and reached out. When his hand touched her upper arm, she felt like she'd been shocked and she pulled away from him ever so slightly. "Here," he took hold of her arm again and gestured to a bench inside the shop, "why don't you have a seat. I'll get you something to drink."

She could barely nod at him as he set her down on the bench, but she did manage to say, "Thank you."

He rewarded her with a smile over his shoulder. "You just relax okay?"

He stepped out of the room and Blake prayed that she could melt into the ground and disappear. He'd touched her and she had actually shrugged him off.

What a dork!

At least he didn't run screaming in the other direction.

And when he'd said little, it wasn't about her size... at least not in the way that other people said it. Like the people who sneer 'tiny' at the big guy, or 'brave' at the person cowering in the corner. He'd said the word but she hadn't heard judgment in his tone.

Huh.

Maybe the air wasn't the only thing refreshing in Eagle Rock, Montana.

She let out an audible sigh and leaned her head back against the glass behind her.

Maybe things were looking up for her.

That would be new at least.

She closed her eyes and did what he said to do.

Relax.

And it felt good. Too good.

CHAPTER 2

HE WAS PRETTY sure he hadn't been gone long, but the woman he'd sat down on the bench was asleep when he got back. He set the glass of water down on his tool chest and looked down at her.

She looked like she'd been driving for a while, but the rumpled look wasn't bad on her.

Not at all.

As Adam stood there beside the bench, he let himself look his fill. Her hair looked mussed like someone had just fisted his hands in it and let go.

Well, if someone had let her go, they were a damn fool. The way she filled out her clothes left him struggling to hold himself together. The way her blouse had twisted slightly left little to the imagination about how lush and full she was underneath. If he had to guess, and really, he was just torturing himself now, he'd bet she wore plain cotton under her clothes. The kind of cotton that would stay wet to show where he'd dragged his tongue, or between her legs when she was good and ready for him.

Adam dragged in a breath and turned away. He needed to

steady himself before he woke her up. The last thing he needed to do was scare her away. While he liked his coveralls because they covered his clothes to keep them clean, they were also fit well so that she would be able to see what she'd done to him with a single look.

That would be a great first impression.

Second, really. She'd already seen him and he was pretty sure she liked what she saw. Women blushing around him wasn't too far outside the norm, but his reaction to her was the part that shocked him.

The women in Eagle Rock were all beautiful. They had spirit and personality, but no matter how much his sister had tried... and she had, over and over... no one had caught his interest.

If his luck held, this woman would wake up, take the glass of water, and leave.

She was probably heading to a big city like Chicago or maybe New York.

It was only a matter of moments before she would get back in her car and leave.

Her car.

Taking a few steps to the side he saw the VW Bug parked up against the side of the building. Painted a white so flat it looked like house paint, he had to wonder if she was driving someone else's car. It didn't seem to fit her.

Like you know. His mind argued with him. *You said half a dozen words to her and now you're deciding what kind of a car fits her personality. You've been alone too long.*

Adam heard a lilting yawn and looked down and met her beautiful brown eyes with his. "If you're tired, I have a place where you can get some rest."

He saw her open her mouth to reply and then close it again as if she was rethinking her answer. The question was, what was she going to say? Yes? Or was she going to beg off at first and was considering staying around?

Why was he worrying about it in the first place?

Reaching over to the top of the tool chest, he picked up the glass and switched hands before he held it out to her. "Water?"

She reached out to grab it before thinking and then slowed her hand to take hold of the glass but avoid touching his fingers.

Curious.

And confusing.

"My hands are clean, I promise."

The shock on her face was telling.

"I wasn't… I mean… I didn't…" she looked so stricken at the thought.

He'd been wrong. And this particular stumbling block was a good indication that she wasn't someone who could take the darker side of his sense of humor.

"I didn't mean anything," her explanation rushed out. "I certainly didn't think… or mean to imply that you… that your hands were dirty."

Lowering the glass into her lap, she looked down into the wavering surface of the water.

"I'm really making a mess of this, aren't I?"

Damn it. He felt like an absolute jerk.

Sitting down beside her on the bench he set his hands on the wood, all too aware that the fingers on his left hand were within inches of her leg. "I think it's probably me making a mess of things," he tried to catch a glimpse of her out of the corner of his eye. "I'm not usually so tongue-tied." It hurt to reveal that to her, but he'd already made a muck out of the situation that he figured she deserved to hear his ham-handed apology. "Still, I took one look at you and I can't seem to put the right words together to make myself understood.

"I know that it seems weird to offer you a place to lie down and I know I'd sound like a jerk if I said you look tired, but it's true. You do." He rushed on. "But not in a bad way."

Her shoulder's shook with a laugh. "No woman wants to hear that she looks tired."

He thought through her words and nodded. "Yeah, I pretty much suck at this kind of conversation. I left the military to come home and take care of my sister while she was pregnant and you have no idea how many things she threw at my head because I just said... stuff."

Adam saw her eyebrows raise and her head tilted so she could literally give him a side-eye.

"I know, I know. Honestly, I'm lucky to be alive."

She was laughing right along with him and damn if she didn't have the most beautiful laugh. Her eyes crinkled up at the corners hiding the rich cinnamon brown he'd seen only a few moments before. And then she reached up and pushed him with the flat of her palm against his shoulder, barely moving him an inch.

"And you haven't learned by now? She must love you a lot."

He must be crazy, but he reached into his back pocket and pulled out his phone to show her the lock screen. "My sister, Annalise and my niece, Ada."

He saw the way her eyes flickered over to the embroidered patch his sister had insisted he put on his coveralls.

"Adam." She smiled even more. "Named after her uncle, huh? I bet she loves her uncle."

He turned the phone in his hand and looked at Ada's two toothed grin. "I like to think so, but I do know she's got me wrapped around her fingers and then some."

"That's so sweet."

He felt her hand touch his and he held still because in he didn't want her to move it away.

Not yet.

He let a moment lapse before he turned to look. Her hand was warmer than his, or maybe that was just how her touch made him feel. She had tanned skin that said she came from somewhere with a lot more sun, or maybe she went to the beach.

And the thought of her body in a bathing suit made him glad he was sitting down.

"Oh, she's too cute!" Her hand moved and she touched the screen where Ada's hair was piled on top of her head in some kind of ponytail thing that Annalise liked to do. Her palm felt like heaven moving over the side of his hand. Adam had to hold himself still so he wouldn't turn his hand and brush his callused palms against her softer skin. "I'm jealous."

"Jealous?" He couldn't really believe that, but when he looked up and saw the wistful downturn of her eyes, he wondered what he was missing. "Are you okay?"

She drew in a light breath and let it out again, but kept her eyes focused inward instead of meeting his gaze. "Yeah, for the most part. I'm actually in a little bit of trouble."

Trouble.

She could have waved a red flag in front of a bull and it wouldn't have gotten a stronger reaction inside of him.

Adam's stomach clenched and he closed his hand over hers. "What can I do?"

Whether it was the touch of his hand, or the sound of his voice, he didn't know, but she started to pull away. He wasn't strong enough to let her go.

He smoothed his thumb over the back of her hand, keeping an eye on the differences between them. The warm tone of her skin against the lighter tone of his said he spent too much damn time indoors, but he liked the look of their differences and loved the feel of her skin against his.

She made a little noise in the back of her throat and he tried to soothe her again.

"Hey, hey... it's okay. I want to help."

She looked up into his eyes. "Why?"

It was a damn good question. Hadn't he just shot Hank down again when he was offered a job to do just that? Was this fate giving him a big ol' middle finger up?

When he didn't answer immediately, she started to pull away, and he should have let her. He didn't need the kinds of problems that her body language was hinting at, but he also couldn't seem to let go of the feeling that her hand belonged in his.

So he gave her the answer he wasn't ready to give. "You wanted to know why."

She nodded. "Yeah, I walk in here and you're getting me water and asking me how you can help. I don't want to complicate your life. I don't even know much about you beside your first name."

"Well," he smiled at her, soothing her with his thumb across the back of her hand, still holding the phone in their combined grasp, "that's a good place to start, right?"

Her cheeks flushed a little and he liked the color on her. "Right. Adam."

The playful tone of her voice was much better than the hesitant warning of a few moments before.

"And you are?"

Tilting her head to the side, she shook her head as if she couldn't believe he was asking. Again, he wondered what he was missing. He didn't socialize much, but she didn't look like she was from Eagle Rock or anywhere nearby. Then again, he reminded himself, ever since the Brotherhood had started, more and more people were moving to Eagle Rock.

"I'm Blake. Blake Lennox."

Blake. He hadn't meant to mouth the word, but he was just trying to reconcile the masculine name with the curvaceous woman sitting beside him.

And he knew she saw him by the raised eyebrow she turned in his direction.

"Oh," he winced, "got myself in trouble again."

Her laughter was almost a sniff of sound. "Do you ever get yourself out of trouble?"

"Ha!" He laughed. Really laughed. "The only one who doesn't try to lecture me is Ada. And now you know why she's my best girl."

Blake's eyes swung down to the phone they were both holding and she smiled. "I can see that. And that's why the only thing you can help me with is my car."

Car. Okay.

"I can handle that."

The look on her face made him puff up a little, putting him on the defensive.

"I do work on cars for a living."

At least she looked a little contrite. "Well that's a good thing, but you might need to have a bit of magic in you, because with the sounds that thing was making as we entered town, I'm not sure she's got any life left in her."

He tried not to look too smug. Blake, he still couldn't get over her name, didn't know how good he was at his job, but he was going to prove it to her.

Yep, one look at a gorgeous woman and he was determined to prove himself a hero. He really needed his head examined.

"Why don't we go look at it before you have me digging a hole in the backyard for your car."

She laughed again and got up from the bench. "All right. Let's go."

Blake got up from the bench and heaven help him, he was treated to just a glimpse of her backside. Whatever those pants were, he wanted to buy her twenty because the way the fabric hugged the lower curves of her butt made him sit up and notice, in a few different ways.

Blowing out a breath, Adam stood and slipped his phone back in his pocket and quickly used his hand to adjust himself before he stepped outside.

Adam knew he was out of his league with Blake, but he was going to stay in the game long enough that he could make some sort of positive impression with her.

It only took him a moment to get outside and he saw her reach into the car to release the hood. The view was another stellar example of why he was so interested in making a good impression. Some guys were breast men, some liked the ass, but he never knew what would attract him to a woman until he found it.

And Blake hit his list in so many ways. Her eyes, her laughter, and yes, he loved what that untucked blouse could only give him a glimpse of.

"Do you need me to lift up the hood for you?"

Not the hood she was talking about. "No, I think I got it."

Walking over to the car he lifted the hood and stared. "How far did you drive this?"

He sensed her tense up beside him and knew that whatever came out of her mouth was going to be either something vague or not-quite-truthful.

"I got the car this morning in Utah. I guess you could say it was an impulse buy."

Adam turned to look at her, surprised. Her words all had the ring of truth to them. Still, there was something very wrong with the engine laid out before him.

"Did you get it at one of those storage auctions? This thing is ancient."

Oh, he'd climbed up on her nerves again. Even though he wasn't the best at reading woman, it seemed like Blake Lennox was almost an open book to him, in hind sight.

And at that moment, he could tell that she didn't like what he'd said.

Not at all.

"She's a perfectly good car, but I think I overworked her. You know," she gestured in the air in a vague circular pattern, "like when you get a cramp after getting back into exercise. I hardly gave her a chance to wind down. As soon as I bought her from Mrs. Lawrence we were on the road and on our way here."

"So, you're not just driving through?"

There it was again, that hesitation before she spoke.

"That depends on my old friend. She's tried to get me to come visit a bunch of times, but I was always busy working and fighting for new opportunities. Now that I finally have a chance, I couldn't pass it up."

He leaned further, reaching for a cap and giving it a good twist. Rust came off, coloring his fingertips. "Well, this might take me a while to look at. If it's giving you trouble you may be right, it might take more than quick fix to get her back on the road.

"But you're in town to see a friend." Adam looked at the clock displayed prominently on the wall of his shop, "I can take you to see them and get you something to eat."

"Something to eat?" She lifted her chin to argue the point, but her stomach made its displeasure known with a loud growl that painted her cheeks a rosy pink. "Looks like I've been outvoted."

He couldn't help the smile on his face when she gave in.

"Don't worry," he reassured her, "I'll fix your car. There hasn't been one beyond my superpowers yet."

She turned away and swept her hand over the front

fender. "Okay, we'll see if you can deliver." Blake closed the door with a snap and turned back around.

Adam heard the sass in her voice he shook his head. "Now you've made this a thing."

Blake gave him a curious look. "A 'thing?'"

He nodded, taking his time, considering his words. "You gave me a challenge and I'm taking you up on it, I have to prove myself."

Her expression changed, almost sad... maybe regret.

"Hey," he walked around the fender and stopped within a foot of her so she could see his own expression, "what did I say?"

She shook her head. "Sorry, forget it."

"Uh, no." He didn't know why, but he reached out and tucked the knuckle of his index finger under her chin and held her still. "If I was an ass, tell me."

Blake blinked and tried to turn away, but he followed her, leaning into her line of sight.

"Blake-"

It was the sound of her name that turned her back to look at him.

"There you are." He smiled, because how could he not when this beautiful woman filled his sight. "I'm not trying to hurt you. If I said something stupid, and... I probably did. Tell me."

He saw the inward gasp of air that substituted for a breath. "You don't have to prove anything to me, Adam." Her eyes flickered up to his for a moment as if she didn't know how he'd react, but he just smiled.

"I know, but I want to." He moved his hand and extended his finger so he could lightly trace the graceful line of her jaw. "Call it a guy thing. I've got to show the pretty girl that I'm not all talk."

Shock. "Pretty?"

"That and more," he explained, lowering his hand back to his side, "but I'm trying not to mess up more than I already have."

Her cheeks flushed with color. "Now I know you're joking."

Adam's jaw tightened and a muscle at the back of his neck cramped. He raised a hand and rubbed at it. Trying to wring a happy smile out of Blake Lennox was quickly becoming a compulsion for him.

And he certainly wasn't fighting it.

"Okay. Let's get something out of the way," he gave her a pointed look, "I mean what I say. I don't just say things to make people feel better. It would be easier if I did, but I don't. That doesn't mean that I know who to explain myself clearly. I know my mother and then my sister tried to teach me." He waited for some kind of reaction and got it. A little nod of her head. "So, here's what we're going to do."

She watched him like she wasn't quite sure where this was going. Thank goodness he did.

He was going to develop a little trust between them, because he couldn't stand the idea of Blake doubting him, even though he knew that meant he'd probably gone a little crazy.

But as long as Blake Lennox remained close enough that he could see the way she swept her tongue over the lush curve of her bottom lip, he was fine with being a little off his rocker.

"You said you came to visit a friend."

Her eyes brightened at his words and he continued.

"Since your car isn't working, will you let me take you to see them? Pretty sure I know everyone who lives within twenty miles." He saw her blush deepen.

"Well, I was going to have to ask you for directions any way. I didn't bring my phone and the only map that shows

Eagle Rock just shows the town as a dot on the road, nothing street level." He gave her a nod hoping that she would continue. "She's not even expecting me, so this might be a mistake."

He had to admit how relieved he was that she hadn't told him no, so he decided to keep her talking.

"I doubt it. Folks around here drop in on each other all the time. It's no big deal when it comes to friends."

He reached up to the top snap on his coveralls and she raised her hands between them. "Whoa, cowboy, what are you doing?"

He didn't stop, opening three snaps before she visibly relaxed and he guessed she must have seen his t-shirt. Less than a minute later he bent down to remove his work boots.

Turning his head to look at her, he enjoyed the rosy flush that made her face a pretty rosy pink. "So, Blake Lennox, who is your friend in Eagle Rock?"

She wrapped her arms around herself as if she wasn't sure she should answer and he started to wonder if the friend she was going to see was a boyfriend. And he wasn't ready to hear that either.

But he offered to give her a ride and he was trying to prove his word to her, so he was stuck.

"Sadie Patterson."

Yep, the fates were trying to kick him square in the back-side. It was a good thing he was already bent over.

"Okay," he pulled the overalls off and stepped back into his boots, "let's go see your friend."

CHAPTER 3

WHEN THEY LEFT the main part of town, he heard Blake's soft sigh as she looked out of the windows. "It's so beautiful out here. I don't think I had a chance to really enjoy it when I was driving in. Between the map and praying that Thelma would hold together, I didn't really look around much."

"Thelma?" He'd heard some crazy names over the years. "Where did that come from?"

"Well," she slid a look at him before she looked out the window again, leaning her cheek against the cool glass, "it was an impulsive decision on my part, but it was the first thing I thought of when I bought it." Her shoulders shook in silent laughter. "I got in and said, 'Well, Thelma, ride or die.'"

"Ride or die?" Adam slowed a little and turned to look at her. "Are you on some sort of multi-state crime spree?"

"No." She paused and then added a couple of words that threw him for another loop. "Not really."

Her laughter was forced, but he wasn't sure how to call her on it and not have her clam up.

"Should I take out a loan for bail money?"

"You're giving me a ride to see my friend. That's huge."

She shifted in her seat and it drew his attention to the way her knee bounced up and down. The road was bumpy enough that he hadn't heard a sound.

"Okay," he said the word and saw her visibly relax, but what she didn't know is that he wasn't going to let it go that easily. "Just know that I'm pretty good at solving problems."

She turned and gave him a quick smile that didn't quite reach her eyes. "If you can fix my car then you're already a miracle worker. That's all I can ask for."

Oh, there's a lot more that he could do. He just had to find a way to get past her tight smiles and placating comments. She didn't want to ask for his help and he always liked a challenge.

So, he decided to switch to a different topic and work his way back around.

"How did you meet Sadie?"

Again, he saw her give him that incredulous look that she'd given him earlier, like she didn't understand why he didn't know her name. It wasn't about ego. No, Blake wasn't puffed up like some folks, but she really seemed confused about it.

Oh. Hmm.

"You work in Hollywood."

She shrugged and he saw a self-depreciating smile on her face.

Oh boy. He'd messed something up.

Again.

"I work from time to time. Sadie's always great to film with and she's always the most gracious person on any set. It's impossible not to fall in love with Sadie."

"Hank's a lucky man."

"You know Hank?" Blake turned in her seat to look at him. "How?"

"We were both in the military."

27

He heard her shift in her seat again, but he was ready for what she said next.

"You're one of those under sell but over produce guys, right?"

Adam's eyes narrowed on the road and he felt the skin between his brows furrow. "I have no idea what that means."

"You're one of those 'still waters run deep' guys. You understate everything. So, when you say you were in the military, you say it like you were just some *dude* in a uniform."

He laughed at the surfer tone she gave to the word '*dude*.'

"When in reality you were probably more like G.I. Joe, super soldier."

"G.I. Joe." He shook his head. "You saw the movie?"

She gave him a huff. "I have all the comics," her tone was full of pride, "I've seen every episode of the cartoon."

"Okay," he agreed with a nod, "then tell me-"

"Please tell me you're not one of those guys who's going to make me prove I've seen it."

He gave her a little look and she held up her hands in surrender.

"Sorry. My bad. Go on."

"Then tell me," he paused waiting for her to cut in, and then continued when she covered her mouth with her hand, "who is your favorite Joe?"

"Lady Jaye."

Her answer came out in a rush and they both shared a little chuckle at the speed.

"I can't help it," she told him, "she is the coolest person on the show. She can kick butt and look good while she's pulling the wool over Destro's eyes. Classy and strong, who wouldn't fall for her?"

"So, you like her because you're like her."

Whatever she was going to say fell silent on her lips. "What?"

She sounded so confused, that he couldn't help but smile. "You're like Lady Jaye," he explained. "Strong and classy. And I'm pretty sure you could knock me down if you wanted to."

"Really?" She sat back in her seat, folding her arms over her chest. "That, I'd like to see."

He had to tighten his grip on the steering wheel when all he wanted to do was pull off to the side of the road, wrap a hand around the back of her neck and kiss her senseless.

Oh, she could knock him over all right. And she wouldn't need to lay a hand on him, just her lips.

Her hands... she could put those on him too, but that would be another problem for him. So many decisions. How did she like to be kissed? Did she like to be on top? Did she like-

"Hey."

Her voice pulled him back to the moment and he had to admit that he'd been lost in his thoughts.

"Isn't that the turn off?"

Sitting up, he saw Blake pointing back over her shoulder. Looking up into the rearview mirror he saw the sign for White Oak Ranch behind them.

"Sorry, I didn't see that." Easing the speed of his truck, he edged off the road and made a quick and easy U turn and then turned onto the drive for the ranch. "Good eyes."

He saw the lift of her chin and the slow curl of her lips into a smile. She looked good. So damn good.

Before she could say anything, Blake sat forward on the passenger seat and set her hands on the dash as she stared at the ranch house. "Goodness!"

Adam tried to keep his eyes on the road and off the way her blouse was riding up in the back and showing him the sweet curve of her backside.

He silently growled at himself. What was he doing? He wasn't usually this... this... interested? That was true, but there was something else. He found women attractive, but Blake got under his skin and he was sure he wasn't going to get it out of his system anytime soon.

"Her house is beautiful!"

"You and my sister," he laughed. "She calls it the White House of Eagle Rock and she's not far off. Sadie and Hank are pretty much our first family. Me? I just look at that house and cringe over the size of their heating bills in the winter."

Blake laughed and he saw her sag back against the passenger seat. "That's the practical way to look at it, I guess, but I think I see their story looking back at me. There's a lot of love in that house."

He couldn't help but be affected by the warm and wistful tone of her voice. "Is that what you want? A house that big?"

He saw her nose wrinkle up. "Goodness, no. I'd need to hire maids to keep something that big clean. I don't need a home that big. I'd be happy with anything if I found a man who loved me the way Hank loves Sadie. I could be blissfully happy in a tiny house."

There wasn't time to continue their conversation. Adam brought his truck to a stop a few feet shy of the front steps and set the brake. He pushed open his door and turned to look at Blake. She seemed frozen in her seat. Her gaze focused up at the door.

Reaching over, Adam touched her arm. "You okay?"

"Yeah." Her voice was a tight, strangled sound. "I'm fine. It's just been awhile."

"If you want to come back later, I'll bring you out again."

"No." She shook her head once, as if she had to convince herself that she meant her words. "I'm not going to take up any more of your time than I already have with this visit."

She pushed open the passenger door and hopped out before he could get there to give her a hand.

All he had to do was catch up to her on the steps and by the time they reached the porch, he had his hand on her lower back, gently moving her toward the door.

SHE FELT his hand on her back and fought the urge to lean into his touch. It didn't feel awkward when he touched her. She didn't feel like he was trying to manhandle her like other men had.

Or the others who thought they had to hurry her along because a curvy girl just had to be slow, sigh. What surprised her even more was her instinctual need to tuck herself against his side and see if he was as warm and comforting as she hoped he was.

What was happening to her?

She was going insane. On the run across almost half the country. She needed a place to hide, not a crush. But oh, how she would love to have him crush his lips against hers.

For the first time in a long time she was really upset that she wasn't the kind of woman who could really attract a man like him. A lead actress like Sadie. Being the chubby best friend wasn't fun to begin with, but moments like this made being the 'friendzone' girl really suck.

They stopped just short of the front door and that's when she got cold feet.

Blake hesitated and Adam turned to look at her.

She didn't look right at him, couldn't. Being a chicken wasn't something she enjoyed. The last thing she wanted to do was to see some kind of judgment on his face. Okay, really the last thing she wanted to see was sympathy or something like that.

Blake felt sorry enough for herself. Seeing pity directed at her would push her closer to the edge. Even though Adam had distracted her with a little banter and laughs, she was already wound tight wondering what had happened back in Los Angeles since she'd been gone.

Her only hope at the moment was to see if Sadie would help her, give her some advice on how to handle the storm that was coming.

"Blake?"

Adam's hand lifted from her back and she felt the loss immediately. Then she felt it on her shoulder, brushing her hair back before it settled down enough to give her a little squeeze.

"Is something wrong?"

"Just- It's just nerves," she blurted out, "I should have called. Maybe we should go back and I'll call, but-" She blinked back unwanted tears. "I don't have my phone so I don't have her number," she gasped in a breath, struggling to hold herself together. The weight of her worries was suddenly bearing down on her like heavens pushing Atlas toward the ground. And she wasn't anything like Atlas. She was just Blake Lennox, the fun fat friend to leading ladies everywhere. "I can't-"

The front door opened and if Adam's hand hadn't been on her shoulder she would have fallen backwards with shock. The man that filled the doorway was a real honest to goodness cowboy. He could have been dressed in a three-piece suit but there was something real and natural about him that just from a look at his face she could imagine him sitting tall in a saddle, his gaze sweeping the land.

Maybe it was just fanciful thinking, but it felt right down to her bones.

And when he turned from Adam to look at her, she felt a measure of her worry fall away. She knew that cowboy. And even though she'd only met him once, she knew she could trust him not to reveal that she was here.

"Hey, Hank."

Hank Patterson was someone who guarded his private life carefully, especially because of his wife. He wouldn't want to draw any kind of attention to his doorstep.

"Blake?" His confusion was gone in a moment. "What are you doing here?"

She winced, because what else could she do? "I was hoping to see Sadie?"

"Of course, come on in." Hank stepped back and held the door open for her. "I'll get you settled and go get Sadie. She's going to be really happy to see you."

Shame pinched at the back of her neck. She could only hope that he was right.

A couple of steps in she turned back and saw that Adam was still on the porch.

There seemed to be a kind of silent conversation going on between the two men and Blake's stomach twisted in her gut. She hadn't asked if Adam was welcome at the Patterson ranch. She took a step back in toward Adam and he saw the movement.

Lifting his hand in a friendly gesture, Adam smiled at her. Hank turned his head toward her and smiled as well. She wasn't sure what to make of the awkward moment, but she didn't have time to worry.

"Blake! Blake Lennox, you come here and give me a hug!" Sadie.

Blake didn't speak when she turned around. She couldn't trust her own voice. One look at Sadie's beautiful face filled with joy was enough to make tears well up in her eyes.

The last few days of manic worry, her energy up and down, and her nerves wound so tight. Blake struggled to keep herself together. As soon as Sadie wrapped her arms around her, Blake's knees buckled as she returned the hug, holding so tight that it was probably the only thing keeping her upright.

She heard Sadie's voice crooning to her, the gentle sweep of a hand over her hair. It brought back some dark memories for Blake that she thought she'd buried, only making the tears fall faster.

The only thing that reached her in the depth of her sorrows was Adam's voice raised in anger.

Sucking down a sob, Blake raised her head from Sadie's shoulder and looked toward the sound. Hank had Adam by the front of his shirt, trying to push him out of the door.

It took two tries before she could get her voice to make the climb out of her throat. "Hank, no!"

Sadie's husband kept one hand fisted in Adam's shirt, but he let the other drop so he could turn and look at her. "Did he hurt you?"

"No!" That was easy to say because it was the truth. "Adam brought me here because I asked him." She turned her gaze on Adam, but he didn't look at her angry. He looked concerned. "I'm so sorry."

He shook his head. "Don't worry about me. What's wrong?"

"It's not Adam. Really! He brought me to see Sadie as a favor. He's been nothing but kind to me." Turning to look at Sadie, Blake pulled in a breath and bit into her bottom lip. "Do you think we could talk for a minute?"

Sadie pulled her in for another hug and pressed a kiss to her cheek. "Of course. Whatever you need." Leaving one arm wrapped around Blake's back, Sadie began to walk her through the main room of the house and toward a hallway. A handful of steps later, Blake snuck a glance over her shoulder. Both Hank and Adam were standing beside each other, their hands at their sides.

"Thank you, Adam." Her breath seared her throat like it was on fire. She already missed him. "You were so sweet to bring me here."

Squeezing her eyes shut, Blake turned back to Sadie and met her friend's curious gaze.

"I need your advice."

"Anything you need, sweetheart, anything."

As Sadie continued to walk her through the house, Blake felt a tentative calm settle over her. She knew that Sadie would help her figure out what her next step should be.

Blake knew she was really and truly out of her depth.

HANK OPENED a beer and set it down in front of Adam on the kitchen counter. "You want to explain what all those tears were about?"

"You know," Adam turned and set his elbow on the counter, crossing one ankle over the other, "if I knew I'd tell you, Hank." Wrapping his hand around the bottle he enjoyed the cool kiss of the glass against his palm. "She came into the shop, because her car decided to break down in my lot. When she told me she was here to see Sadie I brought her over."

Hank gave him a long look and took another sip. "Blake seems pretty attached to you."

Adam shrugged. "I guess because I'm the first person she met here in town." He took another drink and set the bottle down only to realize Hank was entirely too quiet. Hazarding a glance in the other man's direction he found himself under Hank's eagle eye. "What?"

"Blake seemed pretty upset."

The thought sobered him. "Yeah. I knew she had something on her mind, but I had no idea what that was about."

35

Adam blew out a breath. "Whoever's responsible for those tears deserves to have their ass in a sling."

Hank almost hid his snort of laughter. "Sounds like you want to be the man who takes care of that."

Adam met Hank's eyes with a gaze full of fury. "No one should cry like that. Blake's a... a sweet woman. She deserves to smile more."

"Sweet woman." Hank sighed. "I guess you could say that."

Adam rose to his full height and stared straight into Hank's eyes. "What do you mean by that?"

"Nothing bad. You don't know who she is, do you?"

Now that got under his skin like a splinter. "Blake Lennox. She works in Hollywood. That's how she knows Sadie."

Hank laughed and slapped the countertop earning him a full-on glare from Adam. "You don't watch movies, I take it."

His expression souring by the moment, Adam shook his head. "I go if my sister forces me, or if Ada wants to see one of those kid films, I'll take her. What are you getting at?"

The look on Hank's face as he pulled out his phone spoke volumes and Adam wasn't sure he was going to like what he was about to see. Still, he knew Hank wasn't a cruel man so it wasn't going to be anything embarrassing for Blake.

When Hank held the phone out for him to take, Adam took it gingerly between his fingers and swung it around. The picture on the screen didn't look familiar. The first person he recognized was Sadie dressed in an elegant ball-gown with a sash around her body like a beauty queen. Standing beside her was a woman with messy hair, coke bottle glasses, and an outfit that was no better than some kind of trash bag with holes.

He looked up at Hank and held out the phone. "What is this?"

Hank adjusted the view of the image and waved it back at

Adam who looked down at the bottom of the image where a caption could be seen.

Award winning actress Sadie McClain in "Beauty Queen Battle," along with quirky character actress, Blake Lennox.

Blake. Blake?

Adam moved and expanded the image so he could see the woman beside Sadie. Someone had done a great job of making Blake look nearly unrecognizable in the image. "She doesn't look anything like herself."

Hank shrugged and gave him a searching look. "That's what I thought too. The first time I met Blake on a set I didn't recognize her from any films."

"It's a crime," Adam felt his back teeth gnash together, "making her look like that. She's a beautiful woman."

"A beautiful woman with a problem. I'm letting you know right now," Hank clarified, "if she needs help, I'm going to offer it." Picking up his beer, Hank touched it to his lips and took a sip. "Too bad we're not working together."

Adam pushed the beer away from his hand and it moved a couple of inches. He didn't like the sound of Hank's tone, but what could he do?

"Hank?"

"Yeah?"

"If she needs help, I want in."

CHAPTER 4

BLAKE LOOKED DOWN at the empty glass of water in her hands and laughed. Even to her ears it sounded a little manic, but she saw the concern in Sadie's eyes. "I'm sorry," she sighed, "it seems like everyone is offering me water. With all that's going on at least I'll stay hydrated."

She felt another tear escape the corner of her eyes and sighed.

"Maybe not, since I'm crying it all out."

"Oh, sweetheart," Sadie sat down beside her and pressed a tissue to her cheek to dry the errant tear, "what happened?"

"I need some time to think things through," she blurted the words and saw Sadie's eyes narrow, "I know that's the conversation version of 'vague-booking' but there's a reason I'm not telling you what's going on, Sadie."

Sadie set her hand over Blake's. "You know what Hank does, right? Remember the trouble he got me out of?"

Blake nodded. "But we both know that Hank did that because of how much he loves you."

Sadie balked at the idea, but with Blake's pointed look she ended up nodding in agreement. "But the Brotherhood helps all kinds of folks, Blake, and you know that I love you like family. If you need help like the kind the Brotherhood provides, you don't even have to ask, you'll have it."

"I don't think it'll come to that, Sadie. I just need a few days to figure things out and it wasn't until I got on the road that I thought of you here in Montana. There have to be a bunch of tiny towns around Eagle Rock-"

Blake saw Sadie's raised eyebrow.

"Tinier?"

Sadie nodded her agreement.

"And maybe you might know of a cabin I can rent for cash where I don't need to give my real name and-"

The door to the guest room swung open and Hank stepped in, ignoring Sadie's unhappy pout. "You both need to come back to the living room."

Sadie opened her mouth to speak and Blake didn't want to cause the two of them to disagree, so she stood and walked toward the door.

She could hear a hushed conversation between the husband and wife as she moved but kept going. The last thing she wanted to do was cause trouble for the couple she loved so dearly.

When she reached the room, she saw that Adam was still there, but surely that wasn't the reason why Hank had called them out of the guest room.

Adam turned to look at her and she saw the open concern in his eyes. Fear crept over her, riding high on her shoulders and up between her shoulder-blades sending a shiver down her spine.

He reached his hand out to her and she crossed the last few feet to stand beside him, setting her hand in his.

Before she could say a word, he lifted his chin toward the television on the wall.

· · ·

"THAT'S RIGHT, STONE," the news anchor addressed her co-host, "word from Hollywood is that two young actresses have gone missing."

THE SCREEN WAS SUDDENLY SPLIT between an image of Zoe Rogers and herself.

"Zoe." She heard something akin to a moan come from her own throat. "What happened?"

"FROM WHAT WE can cobble together from the press release by Megalodon Studios less than an hour ago, the two women were seen leaving the studio together a few nights ago.

"Our request for security footage was blocked by LAPD and we can only wonder what the young up and coming ingenue, Zoe Rogers had in common with the perpetual comic relief and BFF in every chick flick for the last four years, Blake Lennox."

The other co-host shook his head and sighed dramatically. "I hope there's a reasonable explanation for this, Roberta. I'd hate to think that this is a kind of sinister event."

"I know," Roberta added her own ponderous nod into the mix, "but only time will tell. Until then, we're just going to add our voices to the sobering call from their studio. If anyone has information on where LAPD can find either Zoe or Blake, you're asked to call-"

BLAKE FELT like she was floating outside of her body. She felt cold, dizzy, untethered.

"Zoe, oh God."

Someone took a hold of her and sat her down, but she couldn't do much more than try to breathe and stay conscious. Sadie murmured something to her and even though she couldn't shake her head, she managed to grab on to Sadie and told her in no uncertain terms. "No more water."

Sadie didn't laugh, no one in the room did, but Blake still felt like she wasn't quite *there*.

And thank goodness that no one jumped on her demanding answers. She didn't think she would have been able to give them anything coherent as she remembered the shell-shocked look on Zoe's face when she'd taken her home.

"I should have stayed with her." Guilt pushed her further into the seat cushion beneath her. "She said she was okay, but I shouldn't have left her." She turned to Sadie and said it again, this time nearly shouting. "Why did I do that?"

"Do what?" Sadie leaned in closer and tried to grab both of her hands but only managed to snag one. "What did you do?"

"I left her alone and I should have known better. I know what she was feeling, but she told me to go."

"Okay," Sadie wouldn't let go of Blake's hand and Blake was thankful for the support, knowing she needed to calm down or she wasn't going to be able to help Zoe.

Looking over at Adam, she saw the naked concern in his eyes and she felt horrible that she'd dragged him into this too.

"Blake, baby," he closed his hand around her free hand and leaned closer, "breathe with me."

It only took a handful of deep, slow breaths before she felt like she had a hold on her nerves and her thoughts, but instead of turning back to Sadie, she kept her eyes on Adam.

"Zoe is a friend of mine." She let out a breath. "She's been doing her best to work her way up to bigger projects and the pressure was getting to her. When she came to ask me how she should deal with it we started to meet pretty regularly.

We'd go out for dinner or drinks when she needed someone to listen or a shoulder." Blake sat back and realized she was sitting on the couch. Turning her head back toward Sadie she smiled at her friend. "The same way you used to help me after we did our first film together."

Sadie nodded in understanding. Life in Hollywood could be crazy and many times hurtful and having Sadie there to help her focus was a God send.

"I was just coming back to L.A. after filming in Toronto and it had been so crazy busy we hadn't talked. She called me and said she was getting in over her head with something. She said she needed advice."

"And you went to see her." Hank spoke, his tone even, his expression calm and almost relaxed.

Blake nodded. "I did. I stopped off at the studio and one of the production assistants said I needed to pick up something in my cabana."

"Cabana?" She heard a strange note in Adam's voice and it startled her. Thank goodness Sadie jumped in to answer.

"When I was under contract with Megalodon for a few films, I had a cabana assigned to me." She reached out and touched Hank's hand soothing him with a smile. "It was part of the old studio from back in the Twenties. Now they say it allows for actors on contract to have a little home away from home so that they'll be around more."

"Basically, they want us on call 24/7." Blake sagged a little and barely held herself from leaning toward Adam. This wasn't his problem. "I went to pick up the package and realized it was this thing that the social media division thought would be *fun*." She couldn't help the way she said the word. She'd argued against the idea until she was blue in the face, but it didn't matter. "A video camera in my glasses for the next movie. So, they can have behind the scenes content for the DVD. I put them on and went to go find Zoe because she hadn't called me back, I had to get used to the glasses anyway.

"Her cabana was just a couple down from mine and I saw her light on so I walked up to the door and opened it." Blake swallowed and squeezed her eyes shut. She didn't want to see what the others were thinking. "Seth was there."

"Seth?"

Sadie answered Hank. "Coleman. He owns the studio. He used to be an executive producer on a number of films and when he made billions on the *Outset* trilogy, he bought Peak Studios and renamed it Megalodon."

"Probably because he's a megalomaniac." She heard Adam's deep resonant tone and Blake felt her throat tightening up.

"He was touching her."

The room around her went eerily silent and the panic she'd been trying to tamp down came bubbling up.

Blindly, she reached out her hand and Adam took it in his hand, holding her steady.

"She was on the couch and Seth had his... had his leg in between hers, his hand in her blouse. She was pushing him, trying to move him back but he wouldn't move. He's not big, but he was big enough to hold her down. And then he said, 'You want that movie, don't you?'"

Blake fought off the panic that was climbing up her back with claws. It wasn't her. This was about Zoe.

"And I couldn't let him do that. Zoe didn't deserve it."

Sadie's hand wrapped around her arm. "No one deserves it, Blake. You know that, right?"

She nodded but didn't answer Sadie. That was something she wasn't ready to address on her own, let alone in front of other people. Especially in front of Adam. No one wanted to look like a wimp in front of someone they were attracted too, no matter how impossible it was between them.

"Seth told me to leave, told me it was in my best interest to turn around and forget what I'd seen.

"But I couldn't." Blake reached up her hand, and Sadie's warm reassuring grasp fell away. "I wasn't going to turn my back on Zoe. Not when I could do something." Swallowing didn't do much against the lump in her throat. "I couldn't get him off of her, but I held him back long enough for her to get off the couch."

An old memory reared up and threatened to pull her under. So much for being a strong independent woman, right? Overwhelmed wasn't something she wanted to be anymore. She'd certainly had her share of therapy and it worked for most things, but moments like this, when she could almost feel his skin against hers, it was everything she could do to put a few words together and not break down into tears again.

"He told me that if I said anything... anything about what I saw, he would make sure that I never worked again. That didn't matter to me, you know. Right at that moment, it was so damn obvious that it didn't matter, because it was about Zoe. Because silence wasn't going to stop him. I could see clearly. Right then. It wasn't going to end, unless we did something to stop it."

Adam's hand tightened around hers, but it didn't hurt.

He didn't hurt her.

It was a reassuring feeling, full of warmth and still managed to be gentle.

She couldn't manage to look at him, not yet. Turning toward Sadie she saw the sympathy in her friend's eyes instead of pity. That, she couldn't take.

"Once we were outside, Zoe told me she was going to drive home, but I couldn't let her do that. She was shaking like a leaf. I took her to my car and we left the studio together.

"For a while I was worried that security wouldn't let us leave. Seth controls everything at Megalodon. He could easily have kept us there." Her gaze turned to Hank, begging him to understand. "I tried to talk to her about going to the police. Tried to tell her that Seth couldn't do that to her. He should face consequences for what he'd done.

"But she told me it wasn't the first time. That she'd told her agent, wanted him to help her."

Hank huffed at the words. "He didn't?"

"Even now in this 'modern era' they're still telling women that they have to pay their dues in Hollywood."

"Did you?"

Oh God. Placing what she hoped would be a placid smile on her face, Blake turned to Adam and barely met his eyes.

"Who did it?"

There was a cold edge to Adam's voice, but she knew it wasn't directed toward her.

"Who touched you?"

Sadie set a hand on Blake's knee and tried to derail the question. "Adam, maybe this isn't the time."

Blake jumped on that bandwagon. "The problem here is Zoe. I took her home and we talked in her apartment for a while. I told her I would go with her to file the report. And yes, I would fill out my own."

Adam shifted closer on the couch and held her hand in both of his. He looked like he was going to say something, but she couldn't let him. Not just then. She'd already admitted the truth even though she hadn't done it in so many words, but this wasn't about her.

"I offered to stay with her, sleep on her couch, or even outside in my car. But she told me she needed some time alone to think." I sent her a text when I got home to tell her I'd support her no matter what she decided to do, but I was going to report it. I'd kept silent too long and it was weighing on me, playing havoc on my anxiety." Blake found a smile, for herself. "And that seemed to help her relax a little."

"Did you report it?" Sadie turned her head with her question. "I would have thought that the gossip rags would have been all over that."

"They would have," Blake explained while her mood took a deep downturn, "if I had reported it." Blake tried to pull her hand away from Adam, but he didn't let go. "I went to the police substation closest to my house and I took a moment to get my thoughts... and my courage together but before I opened the door, something across the street caught my eye."

Adam drew her attention as he rubbed his hands against hers. The look he gave her was filled with concern. "Your hands are freezing, baby."

Baby. Goodness. Did he have to be so nonchalant about using words like that? She was already on edge. Somehow hearing that word directed to her was doing dangerous things to her heart. Other men had said that and more but it had never affected her like this.

Never.

"It's like I'm back there," she told him, "sitting in my car with my purse in my hand and my keys in the other, but there was no way I could get out of the car. Lurch was there."

She saw Hank's expression out of the corner of her eye, but she didn't blame him for looking at her like she'd seen a ghost.

"Lurch is just one of the names people have for Seth's personal security. He's tall, but nowhere near as gaunt as the character in the Addams Family."

Hank nodded. "So, Coleman sent his henchman over to warn you away?"

"He must have. It wasn't like Lurch could ever blend in. I don't think he was going to try to do anything more than just be visible."

"Of course they'd do that," Sadie agreed, "try to keep you from going in."

"Well," Blake grudgingly admitted, "it worked. I started up my car and headed over to Zoe's place to make sure she was okay. She wouldn't answer the door but she answered her phone. She told me she wasn't going to report and that I should forget what I saw, because she was going to forget it ever happened."

"Oh, Blake, sweetie." Sadie wrapped her arm around Blake's shoulders. "That must have been hard to hear."

"It bothered me, but what could I do, Sadie? I'd done the same thing. I'd let myself be talked into silence. I told her I wasn't going to give up, that I was going to report it. I was just going to have to go to another station."

Hank and Adam shared a look before Adam spoke. "What made you run?"

She had to take in a deep steadying breath before she answered back. "There was another one of Seth's security guys in a car down the street from my house."

Hank sat forward on the coffee table, bracing his elbows on his knees. "And he didn't see you?"

Blake shook her head. "He was looking at his phone."

"Idiot."

Adam nodded at Hank's assessment. "And you kept driving."

"I couldn't stop. Seth was going to keep trying to frighten me and I wasn't going to let him, but after that I was bordering on paranoid."

"I don't blame you, baby. He was trying to intimidate you. He doesn't sound like a man who lets people go against him. Is that why you bought that horrible car?"

She heard Sadie's curious hum and turned to her friend.

"I bought a car off a little old lady early this morning. She was going to sell it for scrap but I got it working well enough to get it on the road. My car is hidden in her old shed."

"And you made it all the way here," Sadie almost laughed, "you were always good with mechanical stuff." She turned to her husband with a proud grin. "Blake has a degree in Electrical Engineering from Cal Tech."

Blake saw Adam's eyes widen a bit.

"It certainly didn't help me much with her classic car." Blake huffed a little. "It didn't make me happy to have to admit I was going to be useless in fixing it, but it got me here to Eagle Rock, so I'm going to count that as a success.

"But if Zoe's missing and the studio is saying that I have something to do with it."

"That's at least the story they're going to put out there." Hank shook his head. "They're going to try to gaslight the public and force you to come out of hiding."

Sadie started to get up, but Hank pulled her onto his lap. "Don't get upset, babe. We're not going to throw her to the hounds."

Sobering almost immediately, Sadie smoothed her hand over Hank's chest. "I know. I just don't like this. Blake's too sweet for anyone to believe that she'd have anything to do with Zoe disappearing."

"Well, I would have if I could have gotten to her," Blake had to admit the truth. "Still, now that I know they're probably... that they're definitely going to try to make people believe that I took Zoe somewhere, they're going to want to make sure I don't say anything."

"We're going to protect you." Sadie's tone and expression brooked no argument. She looked up at Hank. "She can stay in one of our guest rooms and-"

A child's cry turned Blake's head and she saw the baby monitor on the end table. "Oh, your baby."

Hank helped Sadie to her feet before he got up too. "We'll be right back."

Sadie gave Blake a smile. "You might have to do some snuggle duty once she's over her cranky mood."

Blake watched the pair leave the room and her heart fell from her throat and straight into her stomach. "How could I forget that she had a baby? It felt like she'd moved here just a little while ago. How did I-"

She lurched to her feet, pulling her hand free from Adam's comforting touch. "I've got to go."

Moving around the couch, she started for the door, trying to ignore Adam's voice as he called to her.

When he was almost at her side, she held up her hand and walked faster. "It's better if I just leave and then everyone can go on with their lives. There's no way that I'm going to do anything to endanger Sadie or her family. That's crazy!" She knew she was babbling, but that's the best she could do at the moment.

She really needed a good three weeks of sleep to get her head on straight.

If she could sleep.

And that, she knew, was going to be unlikely with all of this on her shoulders.

"Blake, stop!"

"I'm going to go back to town and catch a ride somewhere." She paused at the door, her hand on the knob and looked at Adam, silently trying to commit everything about him to memory as it wasn't likely that they'd see each other again. "I want to thank you for your help, for your kindness, for... everything, but you don't deserve to be dragged into this."

"Dragged?" He shook his head. "Baby, no one has ever dragged me into anything, just ask Hank. But if you're going somewhere right now, I'm going with you."

Blake knew in that moment that she'd lost her ever loving mind. She looked up at him and it dawned on her. "I'm such a nut," she groaned, "you brought me here. I get it. Sorry," she shook her head, "You must think I'm-"

"I think you're driving me crazy, Blake."

She stared back at him unsure of how he meant that, but before she could ask, he took hold of her hand and drew it up against his chest, just below his heart.

"If you want to keep Sadie and her family out of this, that's fine, but you've got me. I'll see you through this."

"Well," Hank's voice reached them from across the room, "it's about damn time, Adam. Welcome to the Brotherhood."

CHAPTER 5

THERE WASN'T any time to lick his wounds. Adam still had to convince Blake that he wasn't going to let her go. The woman seated beside him in his truck was beautiful and apparently brilliant, but she had this compulsive need to put a wall between her problems and others, trying to protect them.

Hank had done his level best to assure Blake that Adam could kick any amount of ass necessary to protect her, but the curvaceous beauty seated less than two feet away was determined to protect him.

Protect.

Him.

He wanted to throttle her.

No.

He wanted to kiss her. Taste her. Not just her mouth, but every inch of her skin. And when he'd done that-

"How fast do you think you can fix my car?"

Adam let out a breath before he took his foot off the gas pedal and pulled off on a smooth stretch of dirt beside the road.

Once he put the truck in park, he turned on the seat, bending his right knee so he could set his leg on the seat. He looked straight at her gorgeous face and smiled when she kept her gaze straight out of the windshield as if ignoring him was going to make this any easier.

"Let's just get one thing straight, Miss Lennox."

He saw her spine straighten, but she kept her focus down the long road ahead of them on the way back into town.

She was magnificent when she was stubborn. Which he realized was likely to be every moment that she was awake.

"I'm going to fix your car, because I said I would, but you are not going to run away from me."

She turned to stare at him on an open-mouthed gasp. "I'm not trying to run away from you." Her lips pressed together and the fullness of her bottom lip had him hard in an instant. "I'm just trying to keep you safe!"

He could get used to her raging at him. The fire in her eyes didn't stay there, it coursed through her veins and colored her cheeks to a dusky rose. When she swung her gaze back through the windshield, she folded her arms across her chest and huffed out a breath.

He knew then that convincing Blake to stay with him until they figured out the shit show that was happening in Hollywood had a likely success rate of snow on the beach in Hawaii.

It was also the same moment that he realized there was probably just enough room to pull her under him on the bench seat of his truck.

Then again, they could also fit if he got her on top.

And right there was the reason why he was a goner.

Blake Lennox was the only one who could distract him like this. Everyone else in his life had their own place and their own space and he kept them all in order.

But this woman who had literally been in his life for a few

hours, was finding her way into cracks he didn't even know he had and he knew if she was there for any period of time, she was likely to break everything open.

The funny thing was, he didn't seem to mind. He certainly wasn't fighting it,

She was certainly fighting him.

He smiled at the thought and turned on the seat to get both feet back on the floorboard. Setting his foot on the brake he put the truck in gear and started back on the road.

There was an ominous kind of silence that fell between them and her expression and the tilt of her head didn't change. She was going to give him the cold shoulder and all the other parts that went along with it.

And his reaction? It was just another indication that he might have lost his mind, because he ate it up.

He was done arguing with Blake for the moment. He had a feeling she could *out stubborn* him, so there was little left to do than to just say something and hope for the best.

"You know, it might take a bit to fix your VW clunker."

He saw the way her shoulders dropped and her neck seemed to grow another inch. She might think that the car was a certified antique, but it was hers.

"I think there might be some mice nesting in your radiator."

"Really? I didn't notice it." The corner of her mouth twitched, but he didn't let on that he'd seen it.

"And there seemed to be some kind of a bird's nest in your bumper."

She gave it a thought and her shoulders eased the tiniest bit. "Huh, well... I guess we could find a safe spot to move the nest to, unless you're not a fan of nature."

"Oh, I'm a fan of nature," he echoed, and chanced a look over at her, "after all, I can't argue with nature when it created you."

Blake dropped her chin and then turned toward the passenger window.

He had to keep his eyes on the road for the most part, but he saw the pained look in her eyes through the reflection in the glass.

"What did I say?"

A ghost of a smile touched her lips again. "It's just me."

Adam turned onto the main road into town. "I think that whatever you're feeling isn't just about you. I bet there's a bunch of people that put that look on your face."

She tried to hide the look of shock that traced over her features, but she hadn't managed it well at all.

"I bet there were people who were mean to you, Blake. Hurtful. Idiotic. Criminally stupid people."

Her shoulders eased a little more and she lowered her arms. "You say the nicest things."

His fingers itched a little and he didn't even bother fighting it. Reaching across the small gap between them he wrapped his hand around hers. "Don't do that, baby," he felt her flinch, "don't put me in the same category as other people. I'm not them. I'm not going to be."

"So, I'm just supposed to take what you say as the truth?"

"Are you going to lie to me?"

She let out a breath that was halfway between a scoff and a laugh. "No." She snapped that word at him. "I may not tell you everything I'm thinking or feeling at the moment, but I'm not a liar." Her next words were softer, almost a grumble under her breath. "No matter what people say about actors. I leave all of that stuff on the set."

"Then when I say something, try," he saw her little wince, "I said 'try' to understand that I'm not putting on an act." They drew closer to the shop and he had to let go of her hand to signal for the turn. "Give me a chance to prove that I'm not just like *them*."

When they pulled into the lot, Adam pulled the car up behind the shop, far enough back from the street that no one would see them. He touched her leg with a gentle pat, hoping that she would stay in her seat until he came around to get her.

It was almost a miracle when she did just that.

Opening her door, Adam held his hands out and she stepped out onto the runner and reached out to him.

It was a moment that he'd never forget.

In that moment he felt like they'd been in this very position a hundred times or more. Helping the lady down from a train, a stagecoach, a carriage, a horse. Reaching out to him, trusting him to see her safely to the ground.

This couldn't just be the only time he would have her give herself over into his care, hold her securely in his hands.

Adam settled his hands on her waist, his fingers on the rise of her hips, and lowered her down to the ground.

She felt warm against his skin even with several layers of cloth between them. She felt supple and lush.

She felt like everything he'd ever dreamed of and knew he'd never have.

And yet here she was looking up into his eyes with the kind of wonder he felt beating against his ribs.

"I know."

It took him a moment to realize that he had lost himself in the moment. "You know...?"

"That you're not like them, Adam. You're not like anyone I've ever met and that's part of the problem." Her smile was a gentle sweep of a smile on her lips. "You're unfamiliar territory and that's frightening and dangerous all at the same time. You make me feel something I'm not sure I want to, but I can't help myself at the same time.

"So, I'm going to let myself step out on a limb and hope that I don't break that branch with my-"

He stepped in and covered her mouth with his.

It wasn't a hard kiss that pushed her back against the truck. It wasn't a demand for anything.

It was a question, desiring of an answer, and when he lifted his lips from hers, she chased the kiss to his lips.

Yes. She pressed her lips against his a second time.

Yes. She tilted her head to rub her bottom lip against his.

"Yes," she sighed and she felt his hand cup against the nape of her neck.

"Ah-hem! Adam? I hope you didn't ask me over to watch you suck face with- no!"

Adam reluctantly released Blake's lips to turn his head and give his sister a look that told her how lucky she was that she was his blood. "Hello, Annalise."

His sister didn't even look at him when he said her name. She was staring, open-mouthed at Blake.

"You're Blake Lennox!"

Well, great, he thought, d*oes everyone know who she is except for me?*

Blake smiled and reached out a hand to his sister. She probably would have done more if he didn't still have one arm wrapped around her.

"Nice to meet you, Annalise, was it?"

"No," his sister shook herself, "I'm mean yes. Right?" Annalise looked at him for help. "How do you know Blake Lennox?"

Adam stored this moment away in the back of his head so he could remind his sister of the time she totally lost it over meeting Blake and then he not-so-gently peeled Annalise's hand off Blake's.

His sister glared at him as if he'd just taken away her ice

cream cone. "You were going to cut off the circulation in her hand."

That got to her. "Oh my- I'm so sorry, Blake. I mean Miss Lennox."

Blake had managed to wiggle free of him by that time and reached out again, cupping Annalise's hand in both of hers. "Blake is just fine, Annalise. It's nice to meet Adam's sister."

Annalise almost shrieked when she surged forward and wrapped her arms around Blake's neck. "You're so amazing!" His sister looked at him over Blake's shoulder and mouthed. OH MY GOD ARE YOU DATING HER?

He hesitated for just a heartbeat, but that's all it took.

Annalise pulled back just enough to get her hands on Blake's shoulders. "The ladies at the diner are going to lose their minds when I tell them that my brother is-"

"Annalise, stop!"

He was glad he caught her before she could say something that he was going to regret. He wasn't always so lucky.

Annalise had definitely gotten her personality from their mother's side of the family, talkative to a fault. He'd gotten in a lot of trouble over the years because she would just get so excited that she'd blurt things out.

"You can't tell the ladies about Blake being here."

If he didn't know her better, he would have thought he'd kicked her puppy by the way his sister was looking at him.

"If you'll come upstairs, I'll explain everything, but for the time being no one can know that Blake's here in town and they certainly can't know she's going to be upstairs with me."

Annalise touched one pointer finger to her nose and the other at him. "I knew it. I knew it! You're totally shacking up with Blake Lennox." With a shiver of excitement, Annalise pressed her hands against Blake's cheeks and gave her a squeeze. "I'm going to be the best sister-in-law you've ever had."

Adam barely resisted the urge to disown her right then and there. "Anna, focus."

Snapping to attention, his sister made a mock bow and gave him a wink. "Focusing. What do you need? A wedding planner or-" She must have seen the murderous look in his eyes because she snapped her lips closed.

"I need you to remember all those secret agent games you made me play when we were kids." He saw a spark of interest in her eyes. "Well, Blake needs to hide out for a while, just like I told you, but I want to change her appearance so that anyone looking for her wouldn't see 'her' at a first glance."

"Oh, I can do that." Annalise looked at Blake and looked her over from head to toe. "Are we doing Jason Bourne's girl-friend change or Mrs. Doubtfire change, because while I am killer on make-up technique, I don't do prosthetics."

Adam sucked in a breath trying to calm himself down, but Blake beat him to it.

"More like Jason Bourne's girlfriend, but nothing too bright or eye catching. Subtle, blend in stuff."

Annalise nodded as she settled down and looked Blake over again. "I can do subtle, no matter what my brother told you."

He held up his hands in surrender. "I didn't tell her much about you."

"Why not?" His sister stared at him. "Are you ashamed of your blood, or something?"

"Actually, we've only known each other for a few hours." Blake had stepped in again to settle things. "And your brother is being really sweet to help me. But you should know that one of the first things he told me when we met was how much he loved you and your daughter. He showed me the pictures on his phone."

"Aww... he did?" Annalise turned to look at him and gave him a sappy smile. "You love me?"

"I love you and my niece. Speaking of Ada, where is she?"

Annalise gave him a warning stare. "I left her at the Blue Moose Tavern eating peanuts at the bar."

Adam had to take a breath to steady himself, but before he could respond, he felt a warm touch on his chest. Looking down, he saw Blake's hand high on his chest, patting him gently. She wasn't looking at him, just Annalise. "It's been a hard day for him. I've been dancing on his last nerve for the last few hours, maybe we can give him a little break?"

Adam saw the teeny-tiny little space that Blake had left between her thumb and forefinger a moment before Annalise pinched it closer.

"Okay," his sister grudgingly agreed, "I'll try, but just for you. And it'll be totally worth it if you let me dye your hair."

Panic rushed through Adam's veins like the water pumped down a waterpark slide, but before he could say anything Blake replied.

"Deal!"

The two hugged like old friends before Annalise stuck her tongue out at him and flounced away toward the sidewalk.

When Blake turned to look at him, she had a bright smile on her face. "Wow," she shook her head, "how are the two of you actually related?"

"Well," he reached out a hand and threaded their fingers together, "one of us has to be the adult." He gestured to the back stairs that led up to the second floor and she turned, catching his eye.

"So, what's your role in the family, Adam?"

He shocked himself when he laughed. "I can see that between the two of you I'm going to be outnumbered."

Adam saw her open her mouth and knew she was just going to point out the problem in his words and then close it again. He looked back at her. "Why stop now?"

She shrugged as they climbed the stairs beside each other.

"Well you were already outnumbered by girls, Adam, but now you're going to have to battle against a rising tide of estrogen. Be very, very careful."

Hanging his head, Adam reached into his pocket for his keys. "This is certainly going to be an experience."

Opening the door, he pushed it open and gestured for Blake to enter first. When she did, he saw her lift her gaze to his again. "It's going to be an experience," she agreed, "but it's the first time in a long time that I'm looking forward to something."

A voice in the back of his head reminded him that she was only there because she was in a potentially dangerous situation, but he didn't need to say anything.

By the shadows that invaded the bright light of her eyes, he knew she had just remembered the same thing.

When he locked the door, he set the extra lock and the electronic security system that he didn't use most of the time. Now, he needed it to protect what was his.

CHAPTER 6

IT WASN'T until Adam had given her the nickel tour of the apartment that she realized how little room they were going to share.

Oh, it wasn't about the size of his apartment. It was a nice place, but the size she worried about was how she was going to avoid him.

Okay, maybe those weren't *exactly* the right words. How was she going to stay out of his way? There, that sounded a little less like a chicken. A little more gracious.

A little less like she didn't want to be caught staring at him.

Adam Masterson wasn't model gorgeous or Hollywood leading man gorgeous, but she didn't go for those guys anyway. Those guys were entirely too used to being admired for their physical perfection.

But even that was just some kind of veneer. Most of the hot chests and killer asses in Hollywood were more like Captain Kirk in the original Star Trek. An excellent tailor and perfectly discreet body shaping garments did wonders on camera and from there stunt men keep them looking rugged and body doubles kept them looking like gods in the public eye.

Adam reminded her of Harrison Ford in his Indy heyday. While he didn't have that delicious little scar just under his lip, Adam had a scar just along his hairline near his left temple.

Sure, it wasn't big and it didn't have a lot of scar tissue, but she noticed it. And she liked it. A lot.

It said that he'd been in danger and walked away. The old Bonnie Tyler 'Holding out for a Hero' started up in her head right on cue and she almost had to cover her ears, worried that it might actually be audible in the open space of his living room.

He certainly fit the bill. He'd been in the military. She didn't know a whole lot about what Sadie's husband did beyond the basics, hiring ex-military guys to provide protection for people who needed it. She wasn't sure about exactly what Adam had done in the military, but she'd seen a hint of photos on one of the walls, but it seemed a little odd to snoop.

He certainly didn't brag about it, but she found that most guys who did things weren't the ones broadcasting about it.

Beyond that, she had a feeling there was something painful in the memories. When they walked past the photos on the wall he reached out and touched the corner of one of the largest of the frames, his hand lingering for just a moment.

It was almost as if she could feel the hesitation in his movements, a pang of sorrow that she felt echoing in her own chest, settling in beside her heart.

Adam cleared his throat and set down the glass of water on the coffee table in front of the couch. Staring down at it, he shook his head. "I have other things to drink. You must feel like a fish. We keep giving you water. Not exactly anything all that memorable."

She really hoped he'd relax a little. Since they'd entered his apartment he hadn't even sat down for a moment.

Then again, the only seat in the place beside the chairs at the table was right beside her on the couch. And it wasn't so much a couch as it was a loveseat. Two cushions and the arm rests.

"I like water. Besides, when you look like I do in Hollywood, everyone's always recommending these 'healthy' shakes or meal replacement drinks. After a while I really learned to appreciate unadulterated beverages."

His smile, a little twitch at the corner of his mouth, made her blush. Yeah, come get me, *Indiana*. And that thought only served to deepen the color of her cheeks. She could feel the fire under her skin. "So, you take your beer straight from the bottle?"

Blake winced. "No thanks. I'm not much for beer. My dad cured me of that when I was a little girl."

Adam sat down, but he chose to sit on the armrest on the other side of the loveseat. "Your dad let you drink beer?"

"He let me have a sip," she clarified. "And that one sip tasted so bad that I ended up grabbing his handkerchief and rubbing it against my tongue trying to get the taste off." Blake set a hand over her stomach and willed it to calm down. "To this day the thought of drinking a beer makes me ill."

There was a knock at the front door and Adam stood. He kept a soft look on his face, but she noticed the tense set of his shoulders and his no-nonsense movements as he moved to the door. "I thought you and Sadie mentioned some scene you two had at an Octoberfest."

She groaned and her stomach did too. "For that one they gave me apple juice mixed with something to make it bubble in my glass. Even as much as I liked apple juice before that movie, I barely tolerate it now."

Standing to the side of the door he pushed the button on the console to turn on the screen with a view of the landing outside of his door.

Annalise was standing outside, her arms full.

Before Adam could even move, his sister had turned her face to look straight into the camera. "Hey! Let me in! If my arm breaks off from these shopping bags, I'm going to kick your-"

Adam opened the door. "Language!"

She rolled her eyes. "I'm not going to say A.S.S. in front of Ada."

The little girl heard her name and looked up from the little stuffed bunny she held in her hands. Her eyes filled with abject joy at the sight of Adam and she looked back at her mom before she shouted to the room in general. "Donkey!"

All three adults in the room turned to look at the child and thinking this was just the best thing ever, Ada laughed long and hard. "Donkey!"

Annalise gave her brother a narrowed stare. "What did you do?"

"Me?" Adam reached out and took the shopping bags off Annalise's arms. "You started with that remember?"

Her response was a side-eye glance that had Ada looking back and forth between the two.

"You called me an A.S.S. using the real word and my most precious niece heard you and repeated the word before she asked you what it meant. And you," he set the bags down on the small kitchen table, before pointing to the cell phone sticking halfway out of her back pocket, "looked up a picture and told her it meant donkey."

"Donkey!" Ada repeated and clapped her hands together.

Well, as much as you can clap with a stuffed animal in one hand. "Unca Donkey!"

Blake couldn't help the way her jaw dropped and Adam, well, he looked like he wanted the floor to open up and swallow him whole.

Annalise couldn't seem to decide how horrified she should look as she laughed in big silent shoulder-shaking gulps of air.

"That's it," Adam growled under his breath, "I can't trust you with the baby."

He moved closer and swept Ada out of his sister's hands, pressing kisses on her face as the little girl's peals of laughter flooded the room.

The sight of this man with his work-roughened hands wringing such joy out of a precious little girl did something to her deep down inside.

She'd heard the phrase before, read it in a number of romances, and in more than her share of memes, but she finally understood what it meant to feel her ovaries explode.

Dear Heaven above!

Adam Masterson didn't just look like a blue-collar hero to her, or even the amazing Army Ranger he'd been as a soldier.

The man cuddling the sweet little girl before her looked like a father, the kind of family man she'd dreamed about for herself.

Oh no, she sighed and tried not to stare at him with hearts in her eyes. In a few short hours the man had turned her into a leading lady wannabe. The problem was, she was always going to be the quirky best friend and that would never change. When it came to Adam Masterson, she was in so much trouble.

∾

SETH COLEMAN barely looked up when his office door opened and closed again moments later. "You better have some good news for me, Robert. You're already late and I expected you to have company."

He didn't have to meet the other man's eyes to know that he was going to be disappointed.

"Sir, we don't know where Blake-"

"No names, Robert. You never know who's listening."

"We had a man at her home, but he hasn't seen her since that night she took Z- they left together."

Sitting back in his chair, Seth stretched one leg out and tipped the seat toward the wall. "Tell me something I don't already know.

"If you don't have her with you, then you missed her. It can't possibly be that hard to find her. Phone?"

"It stopped transmitting in Las Vegas. I'd like to send someone."

Seth let out a breath in a slow exhale that dried his lip to the point that he could feel the skin of his lower lip tighten. "When did you make that decision?"

Robert stammered aloud. "I'm... I'm sorry, sir. What are you-"

"You want to send someone, but you haven't already done it. Are you asking my permission?"

"There's a matter of transportation. On the road we can have someone there in under four hours and-"

The glass paperweight hit the wall and shattered sending shards of glass across Robert's face.

Seth smiled as the man lifted his hand to his cheek and came away with blood on his fingertips.

"Send the jet. How much time have you wasted?"

He had to give the other man credit for glaring back at him. Oh, he was going to have his ass handed to him later, but it took some kind of grit to turn a defiant eye in his direction.

It was a quality that his father had encouraged in him when he was younger. Giving him a smiling nod before knocking him to the floor with the back of his hand. "At least you have balls, son."

And even though he'd tasted blood in his mouth, Seth had enjoyed the grim satisfaction in making his father lose control.

Robert was too big of a man to fight toe to toe, but that wasn't what he had planned for the former soldier. You didn't punish men like him with pain, you take away their pride, chip away at their masculinity, make them bleed in ribbons not bullet holes. Big men fell by degrees.

And himself?

Seth bit the inside of his cheek until he felt the metallic tang of blood on his tongue. He took pain the same way others soaked in praise. It built up his anger and his need until it burst out in a flash of anger that had left a body count in his wake.

Including his father.

When he met Robert's eyes with his own, he saw the other man's tan skin turn ashen at the look.

"Until I tell you something different, what you need to spend to make this happen, you spend. If you need to take the jet do it. Buy someone off, same thing. We'll fix things later, but until we have both of them where I need them, you do what you need to do."

Sitting up in his chair, Seth picked up the contract that he'd left on his desk a few moments before and turned his focus to the words on the page.

"And I want to hear from you every hour until you've managed to fix this. I don't have to tell you how important this is. One loose cannon is a nuisance, but two? Two become a story once they start talking. And while I can't afford this kind of distraction, it's imperative that you find a way to get things under control."

Robert stood there for a long, silent moment and Seth was very close to giving the other man a good example of how he'd made himself the majority owner of a major motion picture studio at his age.

Still, he needed Robert's various and sundry skills. He could always assuage his particular anger later.

He felt Robert's anger like a palpable touch in the room, curling and uncurling across his skin.

If the hired gun thought he knew what anger was, well, he just signed up for another lesson to learn.

Once the door clicked closed behind Robert's retreating figure, Seth went back to deciding whose dreams to fulfill and whose to destroy with a stroke of his pen.

BLAKE STARED at Annalise's chest, because that was all she could do. Seated on the top of Adam's clothes hamper in front of the sink, she was at Annalise's mercy as Adam's sister cut her hair. They'd decided on a deep mahogany red-brown hair dye with darker tones. It was just different enough from her normal shade to change her look, but not wild enough that it made her stand out. Being background? She had that down pat.

"Don't be nervous."

"I'm worrying about how long I'm going to be on my hands and knees picking up hairs off the tile. The last thing I want to be is one of 'those people' who come into someone's life and turn things upside down." With a little self-depreciating laugh at her own expense. "They say that house guests are like fish... you have to throw them out after a couple of days, but I don't want to make your brother regret helping me. He doesn't deserve that."

Leaning back against the sink at Annalise's unspoken urging, Blake was careful to lay the dark towel down on the edge of the white porcelain before leaning her head against it.

Reaching over, Annalise turned on the water and let it run for a bit before touching her wrist to the stream. "I don't think you have to worry about my bother wanting you out of here."

Blake closed her eyes and tried to ignore the smiling tone of the other woman's voice.

"I think, if anything, he's not going to want you to leave."

Even with her eyes closed, Blake rolled her eyes.

Annalise's laughter mixed in with the running water in her ears. "I'm not just saying it. I've seen the way he looks at you."

Blake's eyes snapped open and she started to sit up, but Annalise's easy touch on her shoulder settled her back.

"You don't see it?"

Blake moved her head back and forth but kept her eyes on Annalise. "See what?"

Warm water rained down over her hair, weighing it down, soothing her shock.

Annalise had her eyes focused on her work, using her hands to direct the flow of water over her hair, washing out the dye. "I have to admit, having your brother lose his head over someone on the run from bad guys sounds like a great movie plot. I mean, you could make big bucks off something like that. The hot ex-military guy," she laughed when Blake's brow creased together, "oh, he's my brother, but even I know he's hot. Lord knows I hear the women in the diner talking about him." Leaning closer, Annalise's voice became barely a whisper. "I think a few of them have brought their cars in for a repair when there wasn't even a problem. No bites."

Blake lifted her hand and touched the side of her neck and then rolled her shoulder when she'd realized what she'd done. Yes, her mind went there.

She certainly didn't blame those women. If she wasn't in the middle of the craziest moment in her life, she would have found herself staring at the very least. Okay, ogling. No, that didn't sound any better.

"But you said he looks at me."

Oh, smooth. Really smooth. Like eighth grade, pass-a-note-in-class kind of smooth.

The good thing was that Annalise didn't seem to care.

"Like the moment he saw his first custom Harley." She grinned and continued to wash the excess dye from her hair, pausing at times to use her fingers to separate the lengths that she'd cut. "And just so you know, he's not a player. The man's almost a monk in this town. And like I said," she shut off the water and squeezed out the excess water from Blake's hair, "he's into you."

Blake wrapped the towel up around her head and hair as Annalise helped her sit up.

"I can't say that I wouldn't enjoy seeing my older brother get wrapped around your little finger. He's entirely too much of a rock for my own good. Adam needs to relax a little, smile a little. I think you might be just the thing that takes a little starch out of his jeans."

"I don't know what to say to that." And it was so true. Adam? If wishes were horses, she would have had a whole herd by now. "This is just a temporary thing. I'm not even planning to stay here long. I just need to figure out a way out of this. Find Zoe, get her some help. Report that… that…"

"Douche bag?"

Smiling, Blake gave an emphatic nod. "Yes, exactly.

Report the douche bag and get him locked up. After that it's back to work."

When Annalise didn't say anything in reply, Blake looked up, worried that she'd said the wrong thing.

That was her default setting after all.

But... when she met Annalise's curious gaze, all she saw was a knowing look and a tilted smirk.

"Well, I know that my brother doesn't have a hair dryer. Have you seen his hair?" Annalise shuddered. "Like I said, he's all too strait-laced for his own good. "How about I just rub it out and-"

The peal of a cell phone stopped Annalise cold.

"Oh damn."

Blake reached up to tighten the makeshift towel turban on top of her head. "Something wrong?"

"One sec. Okay?"

Shrugging, Blake sat quietly while Annalise answered the call and made some grumbling comments to the person on the other end. When it was over, Adam's sister gave her a wincing look. "I've got to go. One of the waitresses called in sick and the other waitress is... swamped."

Annalise picked up her purse from the top of the closed toilet lid and made a vague gesture toward the wall.

"Adam took Ada into his room to take a nap-"

Blake stood. "I'll let him know." She followed Annalise into the hall, both of them lowering their voices to help the little girl sleep.

Annalise paused by the door, looking over Blake's hair with a self-satisfied smile. "Your hair should dry on its own. Given the curl I'm already seeing, you're going to look so hot."

Rolling her eyes, Blake smiled back. "If wishes were horses."

Giving Blake a wink, Annalise opened the door and

stepped out onto the landing. "Save the horse, girlfriend, ride the cowboy."

When Blake closed the door, she felt the heated flush on her cheeks.

Right. Me?

CHAPTER 7

BLAKE SAW that the bedroom door was cracked open but she didn't want to call out to Adam and wake up the baby. She crept up to the door and pushed it open inch by inch, hoping that the hinges wouldn't squeak as she went.

Looking over at the bed, the tension in her shoulders eased and she stepped inside.

Adam was fast asleep on the bed, his body a curved wall with his head just under a window and his knees against the wall on the other side of the corner. Along the wall was a whole phalanx of pillows. A perfect protection for his niece…

Who was sitting up against them and playing with her toes!

When she made it to the side of the bed, little Ada looked up at her and the sudden movement tipped her backwards.

Blake didn't have to lean over very far to catch her. Even if she hadn't, everything around the little girl was plush and protective. Still, when she reached out for the little girl, Ada reached back with grasping hands.

"Whoa there, little girl."

Ada was a little thing, but she had a solid body and when Blake set Ada on her hip, she had to gasp in a breath when Ada attached herself like a limpet.

"What's going on, little one?"

Wiggling in her arms, Ada giggled. "Unca sleeping!"

"Shhh…" Blake touched her finger to Ada's lips.

"Shhh…" Ada repeated into Blake's finger, laughing at the end.

Sitting down on the bed in the open space that Adam had left, Blake adjusted the way she held the little girl and smiled at the almost-toothy grin. "You're a big girl, aren't you?"

Ada bobbed her head and the curly ponytail that had been high atop her head started to migrate down over her forehead.

"Looks like you might need someone to fix that ponytail."

The little girl blew a raspberry and Blake blew one right back making Ada laugh hard enough to hiccup. Together they looked back at Adam, but he was still asleep.

"Why don't we try and take care of this."

She set the little girl down on her lap and managed to wriggle the ponytail holder free of the wispy curls and then she worked her fingers through the little girl's hair, finger-combing for a few seconds while the little one closed her eyes and relaxed into her touch.

Oh, how beautiful she was. Beautiful not just in her features but the light in her eyes and her whole-body laughter. Blake tried to remember the last time she had enjoyed that kind of freedom.

After a moment of pondering, she realized that she could count those moments on a single hand and date them all to the time when she had become friends with Sadie.

Her early dreams of finding her creative life in Hollywood were a long-gone memory that had never materialized, but Blake had always been a stubborn girl and she would not- could not- go home.

Blake looked down when something soft touched her forearm. Ada had the ponytail holder in between her fingers and she was dancing it along Blake's bare forearm.

"Ponytail." With a little burst of air from her lips, Ada shook her own head, turning her hair into a wild frizz that made her look like a little Einstein. "Gallop horsey." She continued the path of the little pink elastic hair tie, making little clicking noises as she went. "See?"

Blake did see. How precious was this little girl?

"Silly girl." Wrapping her arms around her, Blake leaned in and rubbed her cheek against that silken shock of curly hair. "So smart and perfect."

"I think so too."

~

HE COULD TELL by the way Blake stiffened that she heard him.

The look she turned to him was a little hesitant, but the impish face that peered at him over her shoulder made it impossible for the awkward moment to stand.

"Sleepy Unca."

"Got me there, baby girl." He pushed up on one hand and moved around so he could get a little closer to the two of them. "She faked me out." Reaching his hand out, he snuck it under Ada's chin and found one of a half-a-dozen ticklish spots. "Didn't you?"

She couldn't answer, shaking with laughter as she was. And the giggling girl tucked her chin down, trapping Adam's hand. He tried to move and withdraw it, but Ada was trapped in her laughter and the movement made him bump up against Blake. He couldn't see, nor was he willing to look down and risk feeling like a complete letch, but he knew his arm was pressed against Blake's breast.

Whether or not she noticed she didn't say anything, she was laughing as well and all he could do was hold on, but a moment later she teetered to the side and leaned her head on his shoulder.

He got a chance to study her hair with her so close. Adam lifted his hand and smoothed a curl between his fingers. "Wow, I just noticed the cut."

She gave him a look that just might have been offended, but while he was fully awake, he still didn't know much about the silent language of women.

"It's good." He let go of the curl and dropped his hand back to his side. Yeah, he'd blurted that out and even his niece stopped laughing to level a look at him that gave him a feeling he should probably stop where he was. But he apparently had left his self-preservation skills elsewhere. "Really curly. Like... like..." He made some kind of idiotic hand gesture near his ears and saw Ada's mouth dropped open and it seemed like she was staring at him in horror. "Like," he paused and tried to keep his gaze off the sweet curve of her backside in those worn black denim jeans against his light blue comforter. That curve.

Inside his head he shook himself, hard, and tried to remind himself that while Ada didn't have a vast vocabulary of her own, she had the most amazing mimicking skills and apparently a little death wish for him.

"Betty," he breathed, "you look like that Betty cartoon, Betty Boop."

Blake's cheeks flushed prettily and her eyes softened. "Well, that's quite the compliment." Then she looked at him again as if she wasn't quite sure. "That was a compliment, right?"

Instead of blurting out an answer, he let her look at him

and see the answer in his eyes first. "I like the way you look, Blake. I really do, but more than that, it's you."

"Me?"

"You," he repeated, "I'm drawn to you. I want to protect you." He drew in a breath and let it go. "I feel an instinctual need to stand between you and the world."

Blake's whole body changed as Ada snuggled in against Blake's shoulder. All the tension in her shoulder's eased and she touched her cheek to Ada's head, her eyes closing as she rocked Ada in her embrace.

She didn't say a word and he could tell her mind was working a mile a minute. And this really wasn't the time to talk about it. Not when Ada was finally falling asleep.

And this time, the little girl wasn't faking it. Her little body looked almost boneless as she cuddled close against Blake, her eyelids slowly drifting down.

"Are we keeping her tonight?"

Blake turned her head slightly and gave him a look. "Her mom was called in to work another shift. What time does she finish?"

Adam looked at the alarm clock on his nightstand. "The diner closes in a couple of hours. She'll probably text me to let me know more."

Blake nodded and continued to rock Ada, humming as she did.

Touching her shoulder, he tilted his head toward the door. "Your back is going to hurt in a bit. I can take her and we can go out into the living room, or you could sleep in here if you like."

He saw the hesitation in her eyes as she looked at the bed and then the door. When she made her decision, he saw a little spark in her eyes.

"I can handle Ada. She's just a little bit of a thing." With ease she got up from the edge of the bed and Adam was torn with moving ahead of her to prepare a space or following, almost alongside just to burn the memory of her into his brain. Seeing Blake holding his niece changed something in him.

Maybe changed wasn't the right word.

Unlocked, maybe. Like the click of his mom's old cabinet when the weather changed and wood shifted. The way it would pop open and let him get into the cereal late at night.

And Blake? The way she held Ada close, smoothed her hair, bouncing her ever so slightly as she hummed... it hit him square in the chest.

A sledgehammer that took his breath away.

He lifted a hand to touch her and then pulled it back to rub at the back of his neck, giving him something to do rather than what he wanted.

To touch her.

To savor the moment.

To feel her soft skin under his fingers. Against his palm.

"Um, here," he let his voice go in a rush, "I'll clear a space on the... on the couch." He met her gaze. "That work for you?"

Her smile was likely for Ada, but when she lifted her chin to look at him, he was lost in the glow. "That's great, we can watch her there."

"Yeah," he nodded and moved on ahead of Blake, and around to the front of the couch, tossing the extra pillows down on the ground. "My sister keeps buying pillows for me. She says that with it only being me here, the couch looks too lonely."

When Blake sat down, she looked at the ground between the coffee table and the couch. "It reminds me of the inside of Jeannie's bottle in 'I Dream of Jeannie.' All you need are some fancy lanterns and diaphanous drapes hanging from the ceiling."

Now he hadn't seen much of the tv show but there wasn't a man alive that he knew who didn't know what Jeannie looked like. Those pants made of that fabric that was almost see through and that top, no more than a bikini, encrusted in jewels.

He bet Blake would look good in one of those.

Really good.

"Is it safe to put her down here on the seat cushion?"

Saved by the question!

"Sure." He chuckled. "Sometimes she sits with me while I'm watching television and she falls asleep."

Pulling the blanket from the back of the couch, Adam laid it down on the cushion and watched as Blake easily laid his niece down on the seat beside her.

"What do you watch?"

"Hmm?" He pulled his gaze away from the way Blake rubbed her hand on Ada's back. "What did you say?"

Her smile raised the temperature in the room a few degrees. "What do you watch on television with Ada?"

Shrugging, he rubbed his palms on his thighs, trying to remind himself that touching Blake wasn't something he could just do. "Whatever was on. I'm not big on kids shows, but there's some half-way decent reality shows. She's pretty good with animal shows but doesn't like people yelling so Bar Rescue and Hell's Kitchen are out."

Blake laughed softly. "Yeah, those are kind of loud, but I'm more of a Project Runway or Ink Master kind of girl."

"Ink Master?" Heat prickled between his shoulder blades. "You like tattoos?"

"Sure!" Turning more toward him, she pulled her knee up on the sofa cushion and leaned against the back. "Some of the artwork is amazing and I like the creative aspect of it. If I wasn't so," she shuddered, "icky about needles and pointy stuff I would get one."

"Where?"

Maybe it was the lump in his throat or the lack of air in his lungs, but hearing Blake talk about wanting a tattoo made him hot. Thinking about her skin and where she might actually put a tattoo and-

"You'd think it was silly."

Oh hell no.

"Try me."

"My hip." She used her fingers to brush Ada's wispy bangs from her forehead and then looked up into his eyes with a blush across her cheeks. "Or rather, near my hip. I'm told the hipbone makes it hurt a lot. So, if I pick a place that has a little more... flesh, then it's not supposed to hurt as much."

"More flesh..." he tried to let out a breath but didn't have one to let go. "Where?"

Her cheeks were almost a brilliant red. "I don't know what it's called in anatomy and I'm not going to point it out."

He shrugged. "Okay." For now.

She went back to humming and rubbing her hand gently over Ada's back.

"You're really good with her. The first few times I tried to hold her she cried," he shook his head, "my sister had to show me how to hold her and even then I didn't do much more than sit in a chair and hold her like she was an armful of C4 explosives. I've never been so afraid."

"It's not that bad," she straightened Ada's dress in the back, "but I bet you got over all of that. Ada certainly is very comfortable with you."

"Mostly." He blew out a breath. "Normally when she falls asleep, I still hold my hand in front of her nose every once in a while just to make sure."

Blake's smile widened. "You're too sweet."

Sweet? That's something no one had ever called him. No one.

"I bet you're an awesome uncle." He swore he heard her sigh and that sound did all kinds of un-uncle-like things to him. "Ada's a lucky little girl."

"You?" He cleared his throat. "Do you have any kids... in your family?"

Her smiled dimmed a bit. "No, nope. Just me. Dad wanted a boy and got me, so that's why I'm Blake. Daughter of Blake and Nancy Lennox."

Adam smiled. "You're Blake junior?"

"Blake, the second," she corrected him.

He held up his hands in surrender. "Yes, your highness."

Ada stirred and Blake smoothed her hand over the little girl's hair and hummed a few notes of a song.

The sound stirred a memory in him and he narrowed his eyes trying to grab a hold of the title in his head. "What... what song is that?"

"Home on the Range." She sighed and leaned her head on the back cushion of the sofa. "It's my go to for years now. Every so often I get a request."

"A request." He was struggling to understand. "Why would-"

"My first job in Hollywood. It was a kid's show. If I had pig tails right about here," she lifted her hands and held them on either side of her jaw, "and a big brown cowboy hat and lots and lots of plaid. Would that jog your memory?" She lifted her shoulders as she dropped her hands back into her lap. "Then again, it wasn't really a show like Bar Rescue, just a little kids' show on PBS, but-"

"Frontier Friends." He repeated the words and slowly nodded. "Annalise had Ada listening to that while she slept." He saw a flicker of emotion run across her features. "Not that I'm saying it was boring. She said it made her calm." He groaned. "I'm sticking my foot in it, aren't I?"

Blake reached out and her hand touched his forearm.

He went still because the heat of her hand made him tense. And it made him hard.

"You're fine," she smiled at him and tilted her head, "It wasn't supposed to be action packed, just a sweet show about a community of folks that help each other. As much as people laughed at what we did, the kids really loved it. Part of the reason why I loved it is that we always had kids on the set." Blake lifted her hand from his arm and as much as he wanted to reach for it and take it back, he watched as she smoothed her fingers through Ada's curls. "Any chance I got to hold one of the kids, I did."

"So," he couldn't believe how easy it was to talk to her, "are you planning on having a whole bunch of your own?"

She cast her eyes away from him, looking down at Ada as she slept on between them. "We'll see," she hesitated in the middle of her answer, "I'm hoping to have a guy in my life first, but if that doesn't work out... I don't know. It's hard to find a guy in Hollywood that doesn't take one look at me and stick me firmly in the 'BFF' category."

He narrowed his gaze on her. "Best Friend Forever?"

"Close, but not quite." Her eyes didn't lift to meet his and he didn't think she wanted to. "Big Fat Friend."

Blake's hand settled between Ada and the back of the sofa, her fingers moving over the fabric on the cushions.

Before he could say anything, she did. "I'm used to it, so don't think you need to say anything to make me feel better. I feel fine."

Even as she said it, the slight tremor in her voice said otherwise.

"No one should hear things like that. Especially when it's-"

"You can't say it's not true," he heard a slight edge to her tone, "that's my role in Hollywood now. I'm the fat girl. The comedy relief. The one lucky enough to hang out with the cool girl. That's how Sadie and I met."

He was processing the idea that anyone could see her as fat. Curvy? Lush? Yes. Fat? That was crazy.

"I can't see Sadie buying into that label for you."

"Oh, she didn't," Blake rushed to defend her friend. "Sadie's too… normal for that. She's one of those people who are completely genuine. She was always a port in the storm for me, and since she's living here in Eagle Rock, I've tried to be that for other girls. Accepting them the way I was accepted and trying to help them navigate the sharks and hippos in the waters."

"Hippos?" That wasn't one he expected.

"There are stories of river travel on the Nile in the Victorian Era where Hippos ripped apart full sized vessels." She winced. "You'll never catch me getting anywhere near hippos."

Laughing, he nodded. "I'll keep that in mind. No hippos for Blake."

An odd moment passed between them and before he could figure out what happened, Blake lifted her hand to cover her mouth, but she couldn't stop the yawn that came a moment later.

"Hey." He smiled at her cautious look. "Why don't you go get some sleep."

She hesitated, looking down at Ada. "I'll wait up with you-" another yawn made her sigh. "I'm sorry." She looked down at the pillows and started to reach down. "I can curl up down there and-"

Adam leaned down and took her hand in his before she could pick up one of the pillows. "Hey." They were eye to eye, less than a foot apart, and the feelings he'd felt when he kissed Blake flooded back. If she wasn't so exhausted and running on empty, it would be a different matter altogether, but more than he was attracted to her and craving her touch, Adam knew she needed her rest.

And rest, she was going to get.

"You've got the bed, Blake. After Annalise comes back, I'll pull out the sofa and sleep out here."

She started to move and then hesitated. "What if she doesn't come back tonight?"

The way she looked at him, concerned, made him feel like he was basking in the sun. How anyone could have over-looked her appeal was beyond him. "If she's too tired, she knows I'll keep her." Gesturing to a door on the other side of the room he smiled. "I have a fold out sleeper for her. I've got this uncle thing down pat."

Standing up, Blake leaned down and brushed Ada's wispy hair back from her face before she placed a tender kiss on the little girl's cheek. When she stepped past him on the sofa, Blake lifted her hand and set it down on his shoulder. "That, you do, Adam. And they're lucky to have you."

He was stunned at her touch and more importantly her words. She sounded... wistful. Before he could shake the confusion from his thoughts she was gone.

CHAPTER 8

THE PHONE RANG and Seth gave the offending object a blistering rebuke before he picked it up. "What?"

"She has a different car. Shouldn't be that hard to track. Plates are out of date." Laughter made its way through the phone line.

"You don't have her." He sat up in the tub and water sloshed over the edge onto marble floors. "I fail to see why you think that's funny."

"Come on, man. She's driving a hunk of junk. I don't see how that's going to get her anywhere but in a ditch. Your problem is halfway solved."

Seth tossed a towel on the ground and stood, narrowing his eyes at the ever-widening pool of water on the floor. "Halfway doesn't mean shit, Robert. Until I have her under control and find out what she's said or done, I'm going to be breathing down your neck."

There was a hesitation on the other end and Seth smiled knowing that he'd gotten his point across. "Yes, sir."

"And the old woman?"

Another pause. "Who is she going to tell?"

Seth leaned against the sink and met his own cold gray eyes in the mirror. "Bathroom tiles are slippery, Robert. And get that car taken apart. I don't want anyone else following your trail."

Clicking off the phone, Seth threw it across the room and listened to the satisfying crack as it hit the wall beside the tub.

"Looks like Blake found her backbone."

BLAKE ALMOST FELL to the floor when she woke up. The unfamiliar surroundings coupled by the rampant nightmares running through her head had her disoriented and shaking. Reaching out she felt the wall above the pillows and let the rough scratch of the brick wall ease her anxiety. The touch was centering and helped her clear her head.

She couldn't quite remember just when she'd left Los Angeles. Everything after the traffic on the 210 seemed like a hazy blur, but sitting here, in Adam's bedroom, felt like she'd fallen down the rabbit hole.

Touching her fingers to her mouth she could feel his lips against hers.

Closing her eyes, she could almost call it back up like a scene from a movie, but one she was starring in... as the heroine.

And if she was any judge... any judge at all... he was into it.

Into her.

She squeezed her eyes closed and rubbed her fingers over her lower lip, but it wasn't the same. She couldn't feel his hands on her. Couldn't feel his breath on her lips.

Her eyes flew open and she scooted toward the edge of

the bed. Swinging her legs off the bottom edge, she got to her feet and moved toward the door.

Blake stopped under the doorframe and looked from the front room and then back over her shoulder to the bathroom. The apartment over the shop had the one bathroom.

Blinking at the sunlight suffusing the open areas of the apartment she knew she'd slept in late and Adam was likely hard at work.

Looking down at her sleep-mussed clothing, she wondered what she was going to do.

The least she could do was splash some water on her face and see what her hair looked like in the morning light.

Entering the bathroom, she realized that she hadn't really looked at it the night before.

At first, she was so focused on Adam's sister and making sure she didn't get on the woman's bad side, and after with Annalise's mad rush to get back to work, Blake had barely had time to notice anything around her. Now, she took a breath and stood in the doorway to survey the room.

Crisp lines of tiny black tile swept the room from one side to the other at the height of her chest and again at her calves. The rest was pristine white and seemed to glow even without the lights on. The towels and all of the shelves were the same bright white as the main room. The only odd colored objects were the toiletries that Adam left on the counters and even those were kept to a minimum.

She would bet all the cash in her purse, all of twenty some odd dollars, that he'd locked everything dangerous away even though Ada couldn't possibly reach them.

He'd err on the side of caution for the little girl, and she loved that about him.

The shower curtain had been left open so she could see the old fashioned footed tub against the back wall, and the amazing handheld shower head that had washed all the dye down the drain.

Blake leaned in to check the bottom of the tub to make sure they hadn't left Adam a mess.

Satisfied, she stood up and pulled the curtain closed out of habit and stopped to laugh.

Not out loud and from her gut but a subtle shake of her shoulders. The image on the curtain was a cartoon pinup of Betty Boop dressed in biker leather and a red rose tucked over her ear.

She'd bet the same money that Annalise had picked out the shower curtain like she'd picked out the pillows and a bunch of other things in the space.

Still, his comment the night before popped up in her head. Maybe he liked the old pinup style, but she did too. She'd always liked Betty's style and her ability to work those heels.

Sighing, Blake turned back toward the door and her eyes caught sight of a stack on a stool just beside the open doorway. She'd missed it on the way in, but it was impossible to miss it on the way out.

She crossed to the stool and picked up the note written on *Masterson Mechanics* letterhead.

B-

Hope you slept well. I didn't want to wake you up because you were out like a light.

Annalise is coming by later to take you shopping. I don't have a clue about women's clothing, so if I made an ass of myself, you can make me pay for it later.

A

We'll get you through this. I promise.

. . .

THE SENTIMENT HAD her near tears. She'd had her share of promises since she'd moved to California and most of them had been empty.

And yet the way Adam had been since she'd arrived, the way he had acted, had cracked open the door she'd slammed closed years ago.

When she'd been backed into a corner... and had her choices taken away.

Snatching up the towels she turned on her heel and headed for the tub.

Pulling off the one sock that had managed to stay on her foot, she attacked the button on her jeans and struggled with her zipper.

"I'm not going to wallow," she grumbled at herself as she pushed her jeans and panties over her hips, "not now. Not ever-"

But she couldn't promise herself that.

Dark and unhappy thoughts didn't have a twelve-step program. Still, she tried to rescue herself when they came up.

It just wasn't possible, not yet anyway, to push those thoughts out of her head.

Too many years of damaging words hurled at her had made it easier to accept the negative, no matter how much she wanted to fight back with the positive. Some things just stuck to her.

Pulling her shirt off, she dropped it on top of the pile and reached between her breasts to unhook her bra.

She let it fall from her fingers to the pile on the floor, but she didn't look at herself in the mirror.

She knew what she'd see there, and she would need all her courage later to go shopping. That was usually just as disappointing as trying out for roles outside of the public's perception.

Setting the water on hot she was surprised how quickly

the water temperature climbed to the perfect setting and she stepped in to rid herself of the grime from the road.

It would have been pure folly to think she could scrub herself free of what she'd seen at the studio. No, that nightmare would only go away when Seth Coleman had paid for what he'd done.

～

ADAM STARED at the electronic readout on the screen and couldn't make heads or tails of it. The most frustrating part of it wasn't that he'd paid a good chunk of change for the diagnostic machine, it was a necessary piece of equipment seeing how Eagle Rock was home to a growing number of folks with expensive automobiles with sensitive systems. The real problem was that he couldn't seem to keep his mind on his work.

His head was filled with things other than working on the Jaguar XJ6 sitting in his shop.

When he'd walked through his bedroom on the way to the shower, he'd tried to keep his eyes focused on the narrow path, but that just hadn't been possible.

He wasn't a man who let his curiosity get the better of him, but he'd already lain awake in bed half the night imagining what she looked like in his bed. The opportunity for a peek?

And what was worse, what was really threatening his ability to focus on the job in front of him, was the fact that Blake Lennox looked better in his bed fully clothed than any woman had ever looked naked… anywhere.

Curves. Lush. Gorgeous. Like Marilyn Monroe. Like Sofia Loren.

Her cheek on his pillow. A hand splayed over his sheets. His blanket tucked between her legs.

He didn't even have to close his eyes to call the image up into his mind.

It was just there.

Living and breathing. The flush of pink in her tanned cheeks. The parted fullness of her lips. The rise and fall of her chest and-

"Hey, brother!"

BANG.

He hit the top of his head on the hood of the car and swore a blue streak.

"Ooh," she hissed, "that sounds like it hurts."

Yeah, well not as much as the aching hard-on in his pants, but his sister did not need to know that.

He'd never live that one down.

"Distracted?"

When he heard her voice just over his shoulder he tensed up. "Don't sneak up on me."

Her laughter grated on his nerves as she walked away a few steps.

"Sneak up on you? I haven't been able to do that in… forever."

Adam tried to avoid her curious gaze. "Yeah, well, this car is giving me fits."

"Oh," she laughed again, "that's another thing that hasn't happened in forever. What's got you- Oooooh!" She smacked him on the arm. "Oh wow."

Adam took a step away. "Leave it alone."

"As if." She took a step closer. "So that kiss yesterday wasn't a one-time thing?"

"No." He shook his head. "Yes."

Silence turned his head and he found Annalise staring at him with narrowed eyes. "No, it's not a one-time thing? Or yes, it was?"

Adam pulled a deep breath into his lungs. "It was… and will be a one-time thing, so just leave it. Okay?"

He didn't see relief in her eyes. He saw a sharper look. Almost angry.

"Why?"

He held out his arms and shook his head. "Why not? She's got enough on her plate and I'm not the kind of guy that would make her happy."

She opened her mouth to argue, but he continued before she could speak. "You're the one who always tells me I'm too closed off. I won't argue with that, because you're right. I came back more messed up than people would think. I cover well, but you've seen it. You've certainly complained about it enough. And Blake's been hurt. She's been treated cruelly. I don't know the details and I'm not going to pry."

"But you're attracted to her." Annalise wasn't going to let it drop, but she did drop her tone knowing that Blake was around somewhere. "You want her."

"Why are you pushing this?"

She crossed her arms and gave him a satisfied nod. "Because I like her. And I love you."

He was determined to ignore the conversation and hopefully push her in a different direction entirely. "You know she was in that kids show, right? Frontier-"

"-Friends." She rolled her eyes. "Of course, but… oh! You didn't?"

Adam sighed. "I don't spend a lot of time watching kids shows."

"Ada watches it all the time."

He nodded. "Ada does. And I," he reminded his sister, "watch her."

"MmmHmm," her tone said she didn't buy it.

"What?"

"Hey."

Both brother and sister turned at the same time and Adam was pretty sure his jaw dropped a good inch at the sight of Blake standing at the foot of the stairs. She was still wearing her jeans, but the shirt she was wearing… the logo of Masterson Garage never looked so good as when it was molded over her full breasts.

Yeah, he was in deep trouble.

"Hey, Blake." Annalise started forward, bumping him with her elbow. "Thanks for saving me a trip up those stairs," she groaned, "I get enough walking around the diner to last me a lifetime."

"I saw you walking across the street and came downstairs."

Adam had to pull his gaze away from the fit of his… her shirt. "You ready to do a little shopping?"

"Ready." Blake gave her back pocket a little pat and he stifled a groan. "I don't know what kinds of clothes they'll have here in Eagle Rock to fit me. I can barely find stuff in Los Angeles that doesn't make me look like I'm wearing a tent or so tight I look like a stuffed sausage."

Sausage.

Yeah, he was going to hell.

Annalise took over where his voice and brain failed him. "You'd be surprised what we have here. Eagle Rock may be small, but we are mighty." Walking over she fished into her purse and brought out a pair of lightly tinted sunglasses. "Here, even with your hair cut short and Adam's old t-shirt on, we don't want people to recognize you."

"I wouldn't worry too much." Blake held the sunglasses in her hands, turning it over and again before putting it on. "I'm mostly invisible, but thanks for thinking of me."

Slipping her arm through Blake's, Annalise gave her a wink. "Oh, we're both thinking of you… a lot."

Adam couldn't do much more than mumble his goodbye,

and just before they turned around the corner of the building, Blake looked back and gave him a hesitant wave.

He couldn't manage to return the gesture in time.

Letting out a breath, he bent over and set his hands on his knees. He may have told his sister that the kiss was a one-time thing, but he wasn't sure he'd be able to live up to it.

He itched to touch her. To hold her.

Blake Lennox was quickly becoming a physical need.

And he was in deep.

∾

ANNALISE WAS ALMOST HIDDEN in the rack of Viola's Vintage Fashions. All Blake could see was some of her hair and every once in a while the gold chain of her purse where it hung off the back of her shoulder. "You know…" her voice was muffled, but still audible, "you've got my brother tied up in knots."

Okay, that wasn't what she expected to hear.

"I'm sorry? What?"

An arm emerged, holding out a fur-edged vest. "Yes? No?"

Wrinkling her nose, Blake shook her head. "No, thanks."

"Yeah, didn't think so." Annalise shrugged and pull the vest back into the pile of fabric. "Seriously though, that kiss you two had going on when I walked up? Hot. H.A.W.T." Annalise peaked out of the rack. "And as weird as it is saying that about my brother," she shuddered, "you have him frazzled, but good."

"Frazzled." Blake had to shake her head. "I think that's sweet of you to say, but no. I don't think so. He was probably just trying to comfort me."

Annalise stepped out of the rack and leveled a look at her that spoke volumes, but she didn't stop there. "Comfort. You." Her eyebrow arched almost into her bangs. "Seriously?"

Blake felt like she was under a microscope. "He was just trying to-"

"Crawl down your throat?"

Her cheeks blazed with heat and she dropped her eyes to the floor. "That's not what he was going."

"Hey," Blake felt Annalise's hands on her arms, "hey… I'm sorry. I'm not trying to make you uncomfortable. Chalk it up to a little sister being a brat."

Blake lifted her gaze and mustered up a smile. "I'm sure you mean well. I just know that Adam… that he was just… acting. He wasn't thinking."

The look on Annalise's face was telling. "Are you trying to stick to the comfort thing? Because if you are, there's this thing called a 'hug.' Adam knows what those are. Hugs are comfort." Annalise dropped her hands down and reached into another rack, pulling out a blouse and holding the garment, hanger and all against Blake's chest. "What my brother was doing was kissing you. You, Blake."

Nodding, she thrust the hanger against Blake and Blake lifted her hand to hold it against her chest. "He was tired?"

"Sure," Annalise laughed, "when he's tired, he goes around kissing people." She picked another blouse off the rack and put it in Blake's hand. "Imagine what he was like as a Ranger. Kissing everyone when he was tired." Laughing she moved onto another rack and Blake followed behind, trying to come up with an excuse.

"I guess… that maybe…"

"Here, try this on too."

Blake looked down at the garment in Annalise's hand. "What's that?"

Wiggling it around, Annalise gave her a look. "It's a skirt."

Reaching out, Blake rubbed the flared hem with her fingers. "It's a scarf."

Annalise looked down at the garment, her lips pursed. "So, it's a little short. It would look amazing on you."

"I'm going to be staying in Adam's apartment until we figure out how to fix things. Where would I wear something like this?"

Narrowing her eyes, Annalise waggled her eyebrows at Blake. "In his apartment until he takes it off you."

Blake couldn't help the laugh that burst from her lips, almost doubling her over. "If wishes were horses," she shook her head at herself, "I mean… or rather, I didn't mean." She felt like her cheeks were on fire. "Annalise, I'm-"

"Perfectly fine." Annalise gave her arm a squeeze and moved on to the next rack. "Seriously. I'm trying to tell you that if you and my brother get together, for whatever reason, I'm cool with it. Personally, I think you guys would be great together. And my brother needs someone to crack open that shell of his."

Smiling, Blake could hear the honesty in Annalise's voice. "He's lucky to have you. And Ada." Blake meant every word. "He's so lucky to have family watching out for him."

Annalise tucked her arm through Blake's and leaned in close to peck a kiss on her cheek. "We're here for you, too."

CHAPTER 9

THE SECOND HALF of the day seemed to go on forever. Blake
kept the television off for most of it. Every time she turned it
on all she had to deal with were more stories about her
missing friend.

Zoe wasn't far from her mind at all. The nightmares she'd
had the night before weren't about herself. No, she'd learned
to live with the memories of that.

All she wanted was to know that Zoe was safe somewhere. Once she knew that, she would head back and stand
beside her friend. In matters like this there really was a bit of
safety in numbers.

The timer on the oven gave out a crisp PING of sound,
and the clock high on the wall told her it was over an hour
after closing time at the shop downstairs.

Part of her wanted to go downstairs, but she didn't want
to push her luck too much. It was one thing to hide out in a
small town, quite another to do it in a town where Sadie was
well known. Her hometown even.

If folks knew Sadie, they might know her movies, and
even with her short, almost pixie cut hair, Blake worried that

someone might connect the dots. She'd already risked a lot by doing the little bit of shopping that she'd done.

And maybe Adam was staying downstairs for a reason.

He'd eaten by himself in the morning. When Annalise had brought her back, they dropped off a sandwich and coffee for him.

That was the last she'd seen of him or heard from him.

All that time just gave her the empty space to fill up, and she did, with worries and worst-case scenarios. The inside voice that had always taunted her took on a new tone. Zoe was in her head alongside Seth. And the words that ricocheted in her head were pounding against her skull by the time the door opened and Adam walked in.

"Hey."

She could only stare back at him as the words in her head echoed over and over.

Adam walked toward her with his gaze fixed on her. It was a look she didn't understand. How could she when she was so confused about her own feelings?

He reached out his hand to touch her and she flinched away.

"Did something happen?"

Did something happen? A pang of panic exploded in her chest, sending her pulse rate racing. Her eyes flickered from the hallway to the door, then to the windows on two walls. When she finally settled her gaze, it was on the small round table near the kitchen. "Dinner's ready."

Once those words were out, she was set in motion. She moved before Adam's hand could reach her and then entered the kitchen, picking up a plate and silverware, and moved around him to the table.

"I thought you'd be up earlier, but I guess you were busy." The plate touched the table with a clatter and she mumbled an apology. "I hope you're hungry, it's been awhile since I cooked but you can't go wrong with a pot roast and potatoes. Especially in Montana, right?"

She moved around him again and picked up the two potholders she'd found earlier and lifted the pan in her hands. Scooting around him she managed to force a smile on her lips. "I probably could have put it on a plate, but I wasn't sure how long you were going to be and I didn't want it to get dry."

Thump. Down on the table.

"Really, I'm not a big meat eater, but I remembered the last time I made a pot roast and I left it uncovered," she dropped open the oven door and reached in for the other pot and dragged it out, "no amount of gravy would have saved that thi- oh, gravy!" Shaking her head, she started to move around him. "I forgot to make gravy, it'll just take-"

The pan was suddenly out of her hands.

"Hey, that's hot!"

Adam set the glass container down on the table, seemingly unbothered by the heat that had been close to searing her fingertips through the potholders.

"Did you burn yourself?" Dropping the potholders to the table top she reached out for his hands and gasped when he took hold of her hands instead. "Adam, don't-"

HE PRESSED her hands against his chest, glad he left his coveralls downstairs in the shop out of habit. He certainly didn't want to get her hands dirty.

She tried to pull away and it killed him to keep hold of her hands, but there was something wrong.

Something that was bothering her and he wanted to help. "Blake, hey."

Blake stopped pulling on her hands, but she turned her

face away from him. He could still see the ruddy color high on her cheeks. It wasn't a blush. She was really upset.

"Let me help."

She held still for a moment and it felt like she was weighing her options.

"I'm sorry, Adam."

He felt a tremor through her hands, but she didn't pull away.

"You walk in the door and I freak out. What a stupid way to say, 'Welcome Home!'"

Her eyes closed and her shoulders sagged just the littlest bit but he felt like the weight transferred to his shoulders.

"Baby," he set her palms flat against his chest and reached out, touching his hands gently against her cheeks.

Her skin was so damn soft against his callused hands. So damn beautiful.

"Baby, you don't have to do anything for me." He moved one hand, brushing his fingertips through the wavy curls that had fallen forward into her face. "You don't have to make dinner. You don't have to do anything at all. You're a guest."

"Apparently, I'm your responsibility." Her tone was tight, but he didn't feel as if it was directed at him. "As if you don't have enough on your plate. A full-time business on your shoulders, a sister and niece to watch out for. I should be helping you, with whatever you need. All I'm doing is taking up your time," her gaze shifted across the apartment, "and a whole lot of space."

He repeated the gesture on the other side, baring her face to him. "You're so hard on yourself, you know that?" Adam couldn't help but smile at her. "I think you'd be the last person to inconvenience anyone. You're not like that. But," he let out a breath and moved a little bit closer to watch her expression carefully, "I know I can't tell you just to trust me.

You've had too many people, who you should have been able to trust, who abused that trust."

She nodded, her eyes watching him with rapt attention.

"Having a friend missing and worrying about them would be enough to have me tied up in knots. Add this guy into the mix. Knowing that he hurt her like he hurt you. Just thinking about him with his hands on you," his teeth ground together and the edges of his vision darkened, "what he did-"

"He didn't hurt me, at least not in the way you think." She swallowed and he worried over her. Her voice sounded like it came through cracked dry mud. "He didn't slap me or twist my arm. He just forced my eyes open to the reality around me. Of me.

"He told me how the world saw me. He told me I was lucky that he was taking an interest in me. That if it wasn't for him, I wasn't going to matter.

"He explained in excruciating detail why I needed his help, his protection. How lucky I was that he could stomach touching me because, if he didn't..." Blake went still for a long moment, but she seemed to sway as if something was twisting inside of her. She dropped her chin to her chest.

"Baby?"

He smoothed his hands over her shoulders and down to her elbows, repeating the gesture.

"Blake, baby, look at me."

When she lifted her chin, she kept her gaze off over his shoulder, but he saw that her eyes were awash in tears. He watched her fighting herself... or maybe her memories. "Can't." Her voice scratched in her throat. "I'm so embarrassed."

"Don't be," his tone was warm and comforting and that only made her cry even more. "You'll never have to worry about him again. Not while I'm around."

"You can't promise that." She continued before he could

argue. "And it's not your battle. I got myself into this mess. I'm the one who wanted this career. I'm the one who let it happen. Everyone has heard the rumors, but I thought it wasn't going to happen to me. I wasn't pretty enough for someone to take notice.

"And Seth said that's why he helped me. That because of who I was, because of what I looked like, I wasn't going to make it without his help.

"But I'm done with this ridiculous dream, Adam. Once I get this taken care of, I'm done. I'm stubborn, but I'm not stupid."

SHE LAUGHED and felt her own cheeks heat with shame. "I've made some hellishly stupid decisions in my time, Adam, but it was like standing on the beach with my toes at the water-line and the tide is coming in.

"Every decision that I shouldn't have made becomes a wave that washes over your toes. It's not bad. It's not really scary. I had my eyes on the horizon, focusing on the dream. I just didn't see the sand eroding under my feet and the next time I looked down, I was up to my ankles in sand and the tide was pulling me under." She felt the empty space in her chest ache with shame. "I did that to myself."

"No." She heard the rough scratch of his voice. Felt his hands grab hers and hold tight. "You don't get to put it all on your shoulders, Blake."

She opened her mouth to speak but the words fell away when she saw the raw intensity in his eyes.

"Men like Seth Coleman are predators," he told her with his gaze fixed on hers, "you say he didn't hurt you, but hurt isn't just a bruise you can see or a broken bone. The words he gave you are more insidious. They're under your skin."

Blake looked down and saw him gently rubbing her hands with his own. The movement was gentle and tender. How had he known how cold she was, when she hadn't even noticed it?

"He slipped his thoughts into your head like a virus. Every word. Every thought. He wanted to poison you with them. And over time he had you believing that what he said was the truth."

Blake heard the conviction in his voice and saw it in his eyes, but she heard other things too. Again, the doubts started to drown out Adam's words.

It was so hard to believe the good. So hard to believe in herself.

"How do I get you to believe that what I say is true?"

"If I knew," she gasped in a breath when her lungs felt like they'd turned to stone, "Don't you think I would have fixed it myself?"

His smile threatened to gut her... cut her to the quick.

Adam held one hand in his solid grasp and brought it up so that her palm touched his cheek. "I hear that fight in your voice, baby, and I know we'll beat him yet."

She looked at him as if he was crazy and yet she wondered the same about herself because she was beginning to feel like he did.

"If you've got that kind of fire in you, we'll burn out all the damage he did. You just have to let me help."

Blake lifted her other hand to set it on his face, holding him still so she could look into his eyes.

"How? How are you going to help me, Adam? What magic wand do you have in your workshop, because I've been to therapists. And let me tell you something..." she knew she was lashing out but she felt like she was suddenly drowning and the panic was real. "I know I'm messed up. I know I'm better than this. I know so many things, but then something happens and I'm right back, in over my head and floundering.

"They say that drowning people will pull you under if you try to help them. So, you better run while you can, Adam. Save yourself so you can be here for Annalise and Ada. I don't deserve-"

"You don't deserve any of this, Blake." He covered her hands with his and held them steady as he turned to place a kiss on one palm and then the other. "I know it's not going to be like flipping a switch. The things that stick with us like this are either the most beautiful things in the world or the things that tear us down."

The energy in the room shifted and suddenly she felt bare under his watchful gaze.

She worked the bottom of his t-shirt from his jeans and slipped her hands under the edge to touch her palms against his skin. Blake saw the look in his eyes change from a deep, watchful concern to a half-hooded, heated look.

An ache, a terrible, crushing ache, eased from around her heart.

"Which one is it for you, Adam?"

She caressed him, a feather-light touch of her fingertips against the hot flush of his skin down to the waistband of his pants and then up and over the ridges of his abs.

"Will my kind of crazy be something beautiful in your life or is it going to break-"

His kiss stole her breath.

His arms wrapped around her and pulled her close, trapping her hands under his shirt.

A second kiss and then a third, brushed against her lips in one direction and then another. Smiling, she leaned into his search and felt his teeth trail along her lower lip.

It was exciting to feel his fervor. The gentle scrape of his teeth, the soothing balm of his tongue, was as foreign as it was addictive. Every brush of her body against his felt like the stroke of a match and soon she was burning to do more than kiss.

It was nearly impossible to speak against his lips, but she found a way to sigh his name. "Adam."

He groaned and curled his body against her, drawing the hard length of his erection along the top of her thigh and against her belly. "Please," he whispered the word along her cheek, "tell me."

Tell him? Lord have mercy, she would tell him whatever he wanted if it meant that he'd keep touching her.

Blake curled her fingers in the tiny space available to her and she felt his muscles contract under the scratch of her nails.

They moved. How? She had no idea.

But one moment she was trapped in his arms and the next she had her back against something hard and his thigh between her legs.

"Oh…"

"Did I hurt you?"

He started to pull his leg away but she hooked her foot around his ankle.

"No," she groaned the word as she leaned into him, enjoying the feel of his hard muscles pressed right against her aching center. "It feels good."

His teeth scraped against the lower curve of her ear and her head tipped back on a sigh.

"So good."

Her hands struggled to grasp his t-shirt, determined to pull it off his body.

"Adam."

He ignored her plea and slid his hands from her lower back and over the swell of her backside.

Then his fingertips bit into the base of each cheek and

pulled her tighter against his body, his teeth worried her ear lobe, sending shivers all over her body.

She ached and he made her tingle. She arched against him and he molded his body to hers.

Adam lifted her a couple of inches and she leaned back, bracing her hands on the counter as he pressed his body between her legs.

As soon as he was close enough, he rocked into her and electricity arced between them, forcing her breath from her lips on a keening gasp of sound.

Another sliding rasp of denim against denim and her eyes fluttered closed.

"Do you feel that, Blake?"

His voice was darker than normal, deeper. Almost a growl.

"Do you feel what you do to me?"

Oh heavens, she felt it, but-

"Don't doubt that it's you, baby."

His hands guided her legs around him before he leaned in, bringing his erection flush against her heat.

"Everything about you makes me hungry for more."

She tightened her legs around him and he pressed tighter against her body. His hard muscle against her softness. Adam rose higher above her as she reveled in the feeling of being drawn under him, falling... but not back against the counter.

Falling deeper into the dream that this... these moments with Adam... could be real.

CHAPTER 10

ADAM WOKE TO A DREAM. As the morning sun fell across the bed, adding a golden cast to the sheets, the light brought out the reddish tones in Blake's hair.

And in that moment, with a deep sense of satisfaction welling up inside of him, Adam lifted his hand from her hip to fan his fingers through her curls.

The thick locks of her hair felt like silk against his skin, covering and revealing them again as he brushed his fingers through her hair again and again.

"So beautiful…"

Blake drew in a deep breath and stretched.

The feel of her sweet backside made his already half-erect dick hard as nails.

When she started to move away, he reached out his hand and set it on her hip, holding her still.

"Oh," her voice was soft and had a light lilt to it, "is that-?"

"Yeah." His hand flexed and it took every ounce of his control not to pull her closer. "If it… makes you uncomfortable…" his voice was rough in his throat.

"It was just a surprise." She set her hand over his, fitting her fingers between his own.

Leaning closer he pressed a kiss to her shoulder. "So was last night."

Even though he couldn't see her face, he swore he could feel her smile as her fingers curled around his. "I'm not used to feeling like that."

He hated to ask, hated it, but he needed to know. "Like... what?"

She shifted a little, moving against him and snuggling closer. "Desired. Needy," she shook her head, "that probably sounds stupid."

"No." He pressed closer to her and felt his cock twitch, pressed tightly between their bodies. "I needed you too. I wanted to be close to you. Against you." His breathing was heavier, hotter as he placed an open-mouthed kiss against her neck. "And when you're ready," he promised, "in you."

Her hand tightened around his, drawing his hand over her hip and against her belly. "I want that too," she hesitated slightly, "I really do, I just... I'm uncomfortable."

"With me?" He stilled, not moving away, but not pressing either. He wasn't going to be 'that' guy.

She shook her head and the ends of some of her curls brushed against his cheek. "With myself. With lights. With you seeing me." Blake swallowed hard. He could see the muscles of her throat working. "I want all of the feelings from last night... and more, but I don't want to see regret on your face."

He moved back and pulled his arm up under his body so he could look down at her. "Hey." It took her a moment to look up at him, but when she did, he saw the reality of her words in her eyes. Hesitation. Fear. And somewhere under it all, hope. And he wanted to feed that hope until the rest of it went away. "Baby, you have nothing to hide from me." Lifting their joined hands, he kissed her knuckles and then settled his cheek on the back of her hand. "If you let me get close enough to you to see you, to touch you, there's nothing you need to hide from me."

"Right," she looked up at him with a look that would have made him laugh if she wasn't serious, "but you're perfect."

Her words hit him square in the heart.

"Don't say that, Blake. It's not true."

Turning on her back, she touched her free hand to his chest. "Looks like it from where I am."

Gently releasing the hand that he held, he sat up and gently traced his hands over her face, down her arms, and over her hips and thighs. "Looks like you're perfect from where I am, Blake." He smoothed his thumb at the edge of her sleep shorts and licked his lips when she let out a breath.

"And when you're ready to let me in," his eyes traveled up her beautiful body to look directly into hers, "I'll show you just how much."

Her eyes, those amazing eyes, watched him, taking in his expression and the way he sat beside her. He wondered if she could see the truth in his eyes, and if she did, would she believe it.

"You've been lied to. You've been hurt. But I need you to know that when you're with me, you get me. I'm just Adam. What I say, I mean. And when I tell you that kissing you last night. Letting me hold you. Caress you and feel your body against mine. I've never been so hard or hungry for a woman in my life. When I say I need you, but I won't take anything from you unless it's freely given, I mean it.

"I'm here and yours for the taking, Blake. You just have to say when."

"Everything is crazy right now." She sat up and he didn't try to pull her back when she turned and set her feet on the ground. "You may think all of this is real," she stood and put a good two or three feet between them, "but it's the situation. You're taking care of me. Keeping me safe. Of course, you're going to feel something for me."

He narrowed his eyes at her. "Is that what it is, Blake? Is that what you feel for me? You just like being protected?"

Adam hated the look that passed over her features, but he had to say the words. He had to show her that her 'logic' was not anything of the kind.

"When you grabbed the back of my neck and pressed your breast into my hand... was that just because you wanted *someone* to touch you? Or was it me that you wanted?

"Because I want it to be me."

She looked stricken and he moved to the edge of the bed and got down on the floor. He was within a foot of her, but he gave her room to move around him if she wanted to.

If he hurt her feelings, he'd never forgive himself, but he had to know. He had to see where her own feelings were.

Blake lifted her hands and gently wiped away the tears that spilled onto her cheeks.

"Baby," he ached for her, "I'm sorry I hurt you-"

"Me?" She shook her head. "I hurt you!" Blake blinked and wiped at her left cheek with the back of her hand. "I didn't think about how it would make *you* feel."

"Don't, please." He didn't want her to feel like that. "I wasn't talking about myself, Blake. I want you to understand that you're the one I see when I look at you, and I like it. A lot. You're the one I want to touch. The one who I want to undress and kiss, and yes, I want to be inside of you and over you and any way you let me, but make sure you understand that it's you that I want."

"And... and I want you too, Adam, I'm just- I'm just... I don't know."

She was struggling to find the words and he wasn't going to let her get stuck in that feeling.

"Then we won't worry about it now, okay?" Adam held out his hand and she took it, her hand trembling slightly. "I've got some work to do downstairs in the shop and you can take the morning to do whatever you like."

He saw her eyebrows lift just a hint. "Downstairs… as in the custom bikes?"

Nodding, he gave her a smile. "I didn't tell you about those, did I?"

She shrugged. "Annalise is very proud of her brother. She told me."

"Okay," he grinned and enjoyed the smile on her face. "Would you be interested in coming down and seeing the shop? You can come back upstairs if you get bored-"

"Oh, you don't have to worry about that," her eyes were bright, "I love bikes. You might have to kick me out of there for distracting you."

A silent laugh lifted his shoulders. "Kick you out? That will never happen." He shook his head. "You want to change clothes before we go down?"

Blake looked down. She was wearing another one of his shirts and a pair of his athletic shorts, filling out both well enough to make his mouth water.

"Yeah," she sighed, "just give me a minute." With that she turned to reach into his closet where she and Annalise had hung the clothes that they'd picked up at the store.

Adam liked seeing her clothes next to his in the closet and the colors that she held in her hand as she disappeared into the bathroom made everything about him sit up and take notice.

He was in deep with Blake, and he loved every minute.

MASTERSON MECHANICS CUSTOM Motorcycles

. . .

THE SIGN on the far wall didn't do the room or the man justice.

There were three motorcycles that were on wooden platforms that showed off the amazing work on all of them. Sure, the paintwork was top-notch, but it was the little elements that made each bike unique that caught her eye.

Blake knew she was probably being rude by staring at the machines in that corner, but she couldn't help herself. Some folks love the crotch rockets, but she loved the older vintage ear-splitting muscle bikes. She'd been on one or two but to be honest what she loved about the bikes were the lines that made them so recognizable and so damn beautiful.

She darted a look over her shoulder. "Can I get a closer look at the Indian?"

Adam's smile was a proud one, but it was his eyes that showed his surprise. "Sure, go ahead."

Stepping carefully between the Bonneville Triumph and the Harley Davidson WL, she reached out to touch the motorcycle that had always been her favorite since she saw a picture of one in an engineering magazine. "It's a Chief!" She stopped her hand from touching it by millimeters. "It's so gorgeous."

She let out her breath in a shuddering exhale that made her cheeks flush with heat.

"Go ahead."

She turned her head to look at Adam and saw a strange look in his eyes. "I'm sorry, what-"

"Touch it." He lifted his chin toward the bike. "I trust you."

Her heart ached in her chest.

The bike was pristine and hauntingly beautiful. The perfection of its paintjob, and the shine on every single metal part was like rays of sun through storm clouds. There was nothing, not a single vehicle in the whole wide world that could compare with this machine. "I don't know," she hesitated, "I wouldn't want to damage it. Or knock it over by accident."

When she looked back at him, she saw the indulgent smile on his lips.

"You are a singular woman, Blake Lennox. Where have you been all of my life?"

Her cheeks were blazing with heat, but she basked in his praise. "I like bikes," she was almost whispering, "but this is an Indian Chief…"

She smoothed her hand over the leather seat and heard a soft groan from Adam.

"The fenders alone are a work of beauty," she drew in a breath and felt the heat from her cheeks work their way down to her throat and down below her collarbones, "all those curves. She is one beautiful bike."

"You're both beautiful." Adam's tone was lower, deeper than normal.

But it was also closer.

When she looked, he stood at the base of the platforms, his hands shoved deep into his pockets. Even with his hands stretching out the front of his jeans, she could easily see the fullness of his erection behind his zipper.

"And someday," his eyes were full of promise, "I'm going to strip you down and bend you over that bike."

There were no words for her feelings in that moment, but her body had no problem expressing itself. Her breasts were heavier, already aching for more of his attentions, her nipples tightening under her bra, and heaven help her, she was wet. It wasn't like she could help it. The idea of this bike and Adam. Adam. Just the thought of him touching her. His bare skin against hers.

And she knew by the way he felt last night, and what she

felt pressed up against her in bed, she was going to love having him inside of her.

"Someday," he repeated and walked away toward the bike that was in the center of the room.

As she watched him walk away, she smoothed her palm over the seat of the bike, enjoying the soft, supple texture of the leather, and how it warmed to her touch. Unbidden, the image of Adam entered her mind. Adam without his jeans and plain cotton t-shirts, bare on the seat, legs braced to keep the bike steady, his hand wrapped around his cock, slowly sliding up and down… his eyes on her.

Her breath slowly blew over her lower lip, sparking a bit of pain that told her she had been biting her lip, hard.

Oh, she would love to see that.

His beautiful body on that equally beautiful bike.

"I'd love to get my hands on that."

"Blake?"

Startled out of her reverie, she turned to look at him. "Hmm?"

"Did you say something?"

"Me?" She lifted her hand off the seat like it burned her and pressed it high on her chest. "Did I? Uh… no. Why?"

He gave her a look that said he knew she was lying. "I was just curious."

Turning her back on the bike and that particularly delicious daydream, she moved closer to his workspace. "What are you working on?"

He shrugged and bobbed his head for a moment. "One of my return customers wants a custom cover on the gas tank. I've been working on the AutoCAD program and the lathe, but there's something that's giving me fits over the fit." He looked up at her with a wince as if he regretted his description. "I can smooth it out after the weld, but I'm a bit of a perfectionist on certain matters…"

"And this is one of those matters." She smiled in agreement as she leaned forward to take a look. "What's bothering you, specifically?"

As Adam described the piece and ran his hand over the area, not touching anything but just showing her the locations, she began to get a better idea of the problem and a possible solution.

"Can I see the piece that you think got the closest to the perfect fit?"

Standing up, Adam moved over to one of the shelves and picked up a metal piece. When he brought it right over and set it in her hands, she drew back a little in surprise.

"What?" He smiled at her, but his eyes shone with curiosity.

"You just gave it to me." When he didn't say anything, she continued. "You're not going to ask me why I want to see it? Or tell me that you'll take care of it and not to worry my 'pretty little head' about it?"

To his credit, he just shook his head and spoke. "No. If you want to see it, you can see it. If you think you can help. Great." He chuckled. "Honestly, you're the only one, aside from my customers that take an interest. Annalise grits her teeth and stares like she's afraid I will literally bore her to death."

"Well, I do like bikes, but if you wanted to talk to me," she drew in a breath and almost missed his eyes flicking a glance at her breasts, "then talk. I love the sound of your voice and if nothing else, knowing that you want to talk to me... makes me really happy."

Holding the piece gently in one hand, she moved to his desk and turned on the magnifying lamp. She turned the piece over once and then again, using the bright fluorescents to observe every inch of the piece that wasn't quite meeting up with the rest of the cover.

"Can you call up your AutoCAD program and the file?"

Adam walked up beside her and started the computer up. When he had the file open, he stepped back and pulled the stool out so she could move between it and the desk. Adam scooted it back a few inches and helped her hop up on it.

His hands didn't leave her hips when she started to work. "I'm saving my work as a separate file."

She didn't speak much as she worked, adjusting the angles and slopes of the design by tiny, almost imperceptible movements. When she had adjusted it enough to give it a real look, she sat back and felt Adam set his hands on her shoulders.

"You might want to try it like this," she explained, "I think the fit will match up a little more."

He leaned forward and she saw his face out of the corner of her eye. "It's different than the adjustments I've been focusing on," he spoke softly as he looked over the design, "but yeah, I think that just might work." He pressed a kiss on her cheek and turned back to look at the image again. "Where did you learn AutoCAD?"

Blake lifted her hand and reached across her body to cover the hand he had on her shoulder. "I have a degree in mechanical engineering, remember?"

"That's right! Sadie mentioned that." He stepped further to the side and turned the stool so she was looking straight at him. "And your acting jobs? When did you have the time?"

Laughing she leaned back to look up at him. "You'd be surprised all of the down time on a set. When we were waiting for things to be set or reset, I'd pull out my books and work on things. It was crazy for a while but it's California and schools understand what it's like to work in the industry and go to school. My teachers were willing to accommodate my crazy schedule and I finished with my degree.

"They also remind me of that every year when they call to ask for donations to the school."

"God, you're amazing."

He leaned in for a kiss and she met him halfway.

Someone with a death wish cleared their throat. "Umm… sorry to interrupt-"

CHAPTER 11

"Umm... sorry to interrupt-"

Adam put himself between their visitors and Blake. "But you're still interrupting." Nodding at Hank, he made sure that his tone was calm because Sadie was there as well. "And just how did you get inside?"

"Uh, that would be me, sorry." Annalise poked her head in the door. "I was coming by to drop off some things for Blake." Leaning to the side so she could see Blake, his sister waggled her fingers. "You'd be surprised how quick Amazon delivers underwear." With a bright grin she gave him a wink. Or Blake a wink. Either way, he still wanted to strangle his sister. "I'll take it upstairs and get out of your hair."

When Annalise was out of the room, Hank drew their attention again. "I'm guessing that neither one of you have been listening to the radio or watching television this morning?"

Sadie reached out and took his hand but directed her words toward Blake. "They found Zoe."

Adam moved to Blake's side and held her hand securely, but as strong as he was, her hand was like an iron vise on his.

"Found?"

"She was found on studio property. We don't have much information, just what the news outlets are saying right now." Sadie let go of Hank's hand and moved toward Blake. "She's gone, Blake. She's dead."

A cry, the kind he'd never heard… and never hoped to hear again, tore from Blake's throat, but she found the strength to get up and wrap her arms around Sadie. The two held onto each other tightly. Sadie, who had more time to accept the news comforted Blake, rocking her slightly as Blake sobbed into her shoulder.

Adam hated to watch her cry.

He hated that he couldn't shield her from the pain she was feeling.

If there was a way, he could have kept the information from her, he would have, but now everything had changed from just waiting this out to protecting her from what came next.

And something was going to come next.

That was the horrifying truth of it.

Before he could think of something to say, Blake lifted her head from Sadie's shoulder and asked her friend a question. "Where?"

Adam shook his head. "Blake-"

"No," she shook her head but kept her gaze on Sadie, "where did they find her?"

He could tell by Sadie's hesitation and her quick look toward Hank that the answer wasn't going to be a good one.

"Stage Eight."

Blake sagged and Adam wrapped his arms around her to hold her against his side. He knew he had to wait for an explanation, this wasn't the time to push.

"That's impossible."

Adam saw Hank's expression and knew that there was a reason for Blake's reply.

"She would never go near it."

Sadie nodded and looked at Hank. "I told you that she'd say the same thing."

"Yes," he leaned closer and pressed a kiss to his wife's temple, "you did."

Adam was rubbing Blake's arm when Sadie turned to him.

"Stage Eight is part of Hollywood history. It predates the new studio name. It was part of the original set of stages built." She cast a worried look at Blake before continuing. "A young woman died there under mysterious circumstances and since then it's been kind of a white whale for paranormal enthusiasts.

"And actors, like most creatives, have a large number of paranormal curious people in our craft, but not Zoe."

Blake lifted her head and looked up at Adam, her eyes fixing on his face. "She's terrified of anything like that. It was a problem for her when she started working for Megalodon. They wanted her to do horror films."

Sadie shook her head. "It was Seth who pushed it. There was some new up and coming director and he wanted Zoe to be the main character, run around a summer camp in a bikini getting blood splashed all over her body."

Adam could feel Blake's anger building as she stood beside him. "But Zoe refused, not that Seth really cared, but he thought he'd show her that it wasn't a big deal and had someone splash stage blood on her as she was walking into the make-up trailer on the last day of filming for 'Love Story.'

"She freaked out! I mean, who wouldn't when you have blood just thrown in your face when you're not expecting it- oh! Sorry." She darted a concerned look to Hank and then back to him. "I didn't mean-"

"It's okay, babe." Adam knew he was speaking for Hank too. "What we saw was because of our jobs. We expected to see blood. Your friend didn't. We understand."

She nodded, but the gesture was hesitant.

"Zoe was a phenom at her arts school. A true artist, but one with a true gentle heart. Something happened to her when she was little and since then she's hated anything like scary movies or haunted houses. After what happened to her with the blood, the studio physician was the one who put an end to it.

"Since then, some of the people on contract have been making jokes about it. Zoe didn't say anything to them, but she knew. If they found her there it wasn't because she went there of her own accord."

Hank's phone chimed and he looked it the screen. "Those 'news' sites are at it again." He skimmed one article and then another, shaking his head. "They're saying that she was found with all kinds of occult items."

"No," Blake moved closer and took the phone from his hand, reading silently for a moment, "not her. Zoe wouldn't. She just wouldn't." She looked to Sadie for support and got it.

"I know, sweetie. I don't believe it either, but it's in the news." Sadie sighed. "Once it's out there it's going to have a life of its own."

"Something has to be done."

Adam heard the tight sound of Blake's voice and knew how much this was hurting her. She had a big heart and loved with everything she was. People saying untruths about her friend would cut deeply into her heart. Before he could figure out what to say to her, she looked up at him.

"Do you mind if I take Sadie upstairs for a minute. I'd like to talk to her, please?"

Adam shook his head. "I don't mind. You know that anything I have is yours."

The only caution he saw was in Hank's face. The married couple shared a look and Sadie again smoothed her hand over his arm before she spoke to Blake. "You know I'll have to tell him later."

"Oh, yes," Blake looked a little rocked by the whole exchange, "of course you would. And I'm going to tell Adam later, I just need to talk to you first. Figure a few things out."

Adam couldn't help but smile inside. Blake had included him in the same vein as Hank. Having her open to him and depending on him, made him feel like a king.

"Hey," he gently caught her arm before she walked away and turned her so that his back was between Blake and the Pattersons, "I'm here for you."

Her smile transfixed him. Took away his breath. "I know."

He set his hands on her hips and stepped just a hint closer until he felt her breath on his cheek.

"And later, I want to make sure you're okay."

Her smile softened, and he'd never seen her so beautiful as that moment.

"Knowing that you care, feels… feels so wonderful, Adam. I'll talk to you later."

He smiled back at her. "I'll be here for you, Blake. Not just today." Adam searched her eyes. "Tell me you know that."

She lifted a hand and set it over his heart. He swore that his heart beat harder against his ribs, trying to get that much closer to her.

"I know that, Adam." She stepped closer and laid her cheek against his chest beside her hand. "And that makes me strong. Strong enough to do what I'm about to do."

SETH SLIPPED OFF his shoes and leaned back in his chair. He'd been hopping since the morning. Even though he knew that they were going to be calling him in once they found the body, he hadn't expected the complete zoo that the studio had become. He knew the officers that were going to be called to the scene, but he didn't expect all kinds of extra people to show up.

Police came out of the woodwork just to say they were on the scene when Zoe Rogers was found.

Then, to add the dripping icing on the cake, the legal office spent all afternoon with him going over all the contingencies of the 'incident.' Those assholes were always so smug. It was almost too good to sit there and know that he was the whole reason why they were shitting themselves over how this would 'look' to the public.

Suck ups, every single one of them.

A knock on his office door had him picking up a crystal paperweight off his desk and test it for weight. It would make a lovely sound shattering against the door.

The knock came again.

"What!"

"Sir? I'm sorry to bother you but I was asked-"

Sitting up, he shoved his feet into his shoes. "Who do you work for?"

"The Social Media Office, Sir?"

He swore a blue streak under his voice before he growled at the door. "Come in!"

The woman who entered the office looked around as if she was waiting to be set upon by wolves. Seth smirked. She would be pretty close to the mark on that.

"What do you want? I'm busy. Don't waste my time."

She looked down at the empty box in her hands. "I am sorry, Mr. Coleman. Missy Price, my boss in the Social Media-"

"Hurry it up."

"I found this box in Blake Lennox's cabana, sir."

That got him on his feet. Carried him across the room. He held out his hand and gestured her closer. "Give it to me."

She set the box in his hand and then stepped back as if she worried, he might grab onto her. That would be later.

Looking down into the box he narrowed his eyes on the instruction sheet inside.

"When was this delivered?"

When Sadie had left, Blake sat down on the sofa and waited for Adam to come up. She was sure it would only take him a few minutes and sure enough, the door to the workshop opened and Adam stepped inside, wiping his hands dry on a clean cloth. "Hey, beautiful."

She smiled at him. How could she not?

"Hey yourself." She gave the cushion beside her a pat. "Want to sit down?"

He moved quickly, taking the seat she'd offered him, but before he was even settled, he reached over and putting his hands on her hips, Adam set her on his lap and wrapped his arms around her. "I was worried about you earlier."

She smiled at him. "Not now?"

Adam shook his head. "You've got this look on your face that says you're ready to take on the world. If you believe it, so do I. I just want to make sure that you know I'm going to be by your side while you do it."

Oh goodness. Hearing it in his voice... if she wasn't already sitting down, he would have swept her off her feet.

She set her hand on his cheek and pressed a kiss to his lips. "Thank you for trusting me."

"Why wouldn't I?" He gave her another kiss. "By the way."

She returned the kiss again, wrapping her arms around his neck as she did. "Hmm?"

He tightened his hold on her and kissed the corner of her mouth. "The new design worked."

She sat up and beamed at him. "It did?"

Adam shook his head. "Did you doubt it?"

Blushing, she laughed. "Not really. I had a good feeling."

He lowered his hands and cupped her backside in his palms. "This is a good feeling too."

"Whoa there, sailor."

He gave her a curious look. "No?"

She flushed under his gaze. "Yes… soon. But right now," she licked her lips because they had suddenly gone dry. "I want to tell you about my talk with Sadie."

Blake appreciated it when he leaned back to listen. He didn't move his hands from her butt, which she really liked, but his focus was on what she had to say. Could he get any more sexy? A man who listened?

"I had to talk to Sadie because she could help me put some of the pieces together about Zoe. I had to know that I wasn't imagining things. If they're floating a story about her being interested in ghosts, they're lying for a reason. And that can't be good. It means they're willing to lie about anything. I can't believe… or rather I was having a hard time realizing that they were going to make it look like Zoe… hurt herself. It's hard enough to imagine that they would hurt Zoe like that. I can't even begin to say the words myself."

"You have a tender heart, babe. You want to think everyone can be good. That they have a line they won't cross."

"But I know that he did this. He had someone do this horrible thing. And he's going to blame it on her. I'm sure of it. I just can't let him destroy her memory too. That's why I needed to talk to Sadie."

"Smart thinking."

She rolled her eyes at him. "You know, if it was almost anyone else, I would think you were just trying to be nice."

"Oh? So, what am I, Blake?"

"You're a really good man, Adam. Probably better than I deserve."

He fanned his thumb across her cheek and she leaned into it. "I'm just trying to keep up with you, baby."

Her expression changed, sobering as he watched her. "I had Sadie call her attorney in Los Angeles."

Well, that got his attention. He sat up straighter. "Okay." He said the word quietly, waiting for her to continue.

"His firm handles all kinds of things and I needed someone who could advise me across the board." She felt his arms tighten a little around her body. "I have a video of that night."

The corner of his mouth turned up in a sly smile. "Those video glasses."

Blake nodded. "Yeah. I had those on when I went to see Zoe." She swallowed and felt the ache in her throat move down into her chest. "Seth is a complete ass. He's a criminal. But, he's not stupid. He'll figure it out sooner or later, Adam. I had to get ahead of this."

"And so, you told the lawyer."

She didn't answer in words, but she knew he saw the truth in her eyes. "We've put contingencies in place, in case I can't get the card myself."

Any hint of a smile left his face. "Don't say things like that."

"I'm a numbers and math girl at heart, Adam. I know what the likelihood is here. And you can hide me here for as long as you want, but that doesn't change the fact that eventually I'll have to go back and face him.

"Go back and get that video and show the world exactly what he is. Tell my story and Zoe's. You won't be able to protect me from the news or public opinion, and there's a chance you won't be able to protect me from Seth and his men."

"Baby-"

She touched her fingers to his lips to keep him quiet. "That's not to say I'll make it easy for him or them, but I have to face facts. And that fact is that I'll have to walk into the lion's den eventually."

"And I'll be there with you."

She smiled, but she knew that it didn't reach her eyes. She'd lived in fear of Seth for too long. Afraid of men like him for too long.

But she knew something else. She knew that Adam would be with her no matter what, because somehow, in just a few days, he was already in her heart.

He was already the reason she hoped that she would end up free of this mess on the other side of this battle.

And while she was waiting, she wanted to take a little something to remember him by when the world fell down around her shoulders.

"Adam?"

"Yeah, baby?"

She looked up and saw him gazing at her with such a tender look in his eyes that she knew, truly, that he thought she was beautiful. That was a memory that she would take with her as well.

That feeling.

This feeling.

Blake set her hand over her own heart and felt it beating, fast and strong against her palm as if her ribs weren't able to protect it anymore.

It was frightening and yet it gave her a freedom to destroy the walls which Adam already lowered since she'd literally found herself on his doorstep.

"Adam," she tried to smile, but only managed a slight pout at the corners of her mouth, "remember when you said I had to be ready?"

His legs shifted underneath her and he drew in one long, deep, breath. "Yeah?"

Drawing her feet closer, she set her hands on his shoulders and shifted her body until she straddled his lap before she lowered herself down onto him.

It was an incredible feeling when she was flush against his body and felt the hard length of him pressing between her legs. A soft, needy moan escaped her lips and she ground herself against him.

When she settled back on top of him, she looked him straight in the eye and told him the words that had been dancing on the tip of her tongue.

"I'm ready, Adam. Show me what I've been missing."

CHAPTER 12

HAVING Blake straddled across him on the couch was like a dream. Having his hands on her hips, feeling the lush swell of her body under his palms was the best kind of temptation. Knowing that she wanted him to touch her and bring her over the edge made him ache with need.

He'd already had his hands on Blake, drunk her sighs from her lips, but the thought of touching her naked skin and filling her up with his cock over and over had him throbbing in his jeans.

She reached for the hem of her blouse and he stopped her. Gently prying her fingers off the fabric.

Adam ignored the pout in her expression. "You wanted me to show you, right?"

He saw the change in her attitude from the pout to a different look entirely. Her eyes challenged him.

Adam shifted a little under her beautiful body and she gasped at the sensation.

Oh yeah, he was ready for that challenge.

"Let me take the reins, Blake. I promise you won't be sorry."

"Reins?" She tossed her head back a little and some of her curls danced around the tops of her ears. "I guess it's because you grew up in Montana?"

He smiled up at her and slid his hands down to the tops of her thighs and back up again. "Maybe it's because I like leather... and I'm still remembering what you looked like with your hands on my bike."

Blake's eyes darkened and he knew where her thoughts had gone.

"Or maybe it's because when you get naked, it's going to be because I took off every single thing you're wearing."

Her breaths came faster, accentuating the rise and fall of her breasts.

Adam moved his hands again, gathering the fabric from the hem of her blouse and lifting it up slowly.

Blake shifted and her hands settled over his.

"Make it fast, okay? Like a band aid."

His eyes fixed on the way she bit into her bottom lip. "Baby, let me take care of you."

She sank down, her thighs spreading slightly, and he felt her heat flaring against him, pulling a groan from his lips.

"You feel so damn good." He lifted the bottom of her blouse and held it just high enough for him to see her breasts loving cupped in her bra. The cream-colored cotton was magic against her tanned skin and as his gaze moved back and forth from one peak to the other, he watched as her nipples began to tighten.

Blake's breath escaped her lips as her hips shifted a fraction of an inch.

He couldn't blame her for wanting to move. He could tell by her heat and the flush of color under her tanned skin that she was aroused. He wasn't the only one who wanted him to take off that bra and taste her tender skin. Adam could already see the tiny bumps forming in anticipation along her skin.

And he was done waiting.

Before she could read his intention, he lifted her blouse up and over her head and slipped it off the curve of her shoulders. He released it when it was just a couple inches farther.

Adam saw her surprise, but he didn't let it stop him. Having her arms pulled slightly back had gently thrust her breasts forward.

Lowering his hands, his fingers traced the inner edge of her bra, the tips against her skin, trailing along the elastic stitching and the fabric.

His hands met at the snap between her breasts and with a flick of one hand it was open. He heard her gasp but couldn't tear his gaze away from the lush curves that he'd revealed. He'd felt them pressed up against his chest. He'd ogled them as they stretched his cotton t-shirt that she used to sleep in.

But he had yet to set his mouth on her skin.

And that, he was going to fix.

Leaning in he used his hands to hold her still as he nuzzled against her breastbone, taking in her scent as she wavered in his grasp. He touched his lips to her skin and felt the fluttering of her heart under his touch. "Blake," he moaned her name as his hands bit into her waist, "I never want to let you go."

He felt her move and smiled when he realized that she couldn't touch him, not with her hands.

"I want to taste you, baby," looking up into her eyes, he saw that they were beginning to lose their focus, "I want to feel you against my tongue."

Another deep breath and the cups of her bra pulled back, catching on the tightened tips of her breasts.

Lifting a hand, he grasped the soft cotton and tugged it to the side, baring the tip of her breast to him.

Before she could let worry fill her head, he closed his mouth over her and swept his tongue over the tip.

She rose up, her backside lifting from his thighs, but he didn't let go. He didn't let her loose as his tongue laved her skin and drew her flesh into a tight peak that tasted berry sweet in his mouth.

The flat of his tongue swept against the underside of her breast and she gasped, pulling away as her hips rocked against his swollen cock. He set a hand against her lower back and held her against him as his other hand brushed the cotton cup away from her other breast until the warmth of his palm drew her other nipple into an answering point.

"Adam."

He looked up and met her eyes. Saw the haze that widened her pupils into dark pools and flooded her cheeks with a warm rosy color. Swirling his tongue around the tight bud he made her shudder and rock against him.

"Adam…"

Lifting his foot, he reached out and dragged the coffee table closer so he could plant his feet down on the worn surface. With his feet up, he lifted his legs and her hips slid closer. The breathy gasp that burst from her lips drew his eyes to her mouth.

Those beautiful lips that he would love to see wrapped around-

Blake took hold of one of his knees and the look that she pinned him with was one of blatant challenge.

"Stop playing with me."

He leaned back and let go of her breast with a pop, his own eyes full of desire. "I'm not playing, beautiful." He chose to prove himself by cradling her breasts in his hands, gently smoothing his palms all over the ripe swells and rolling her nipples between his fingers. "So damn beautiful."

Her lips moved, but he couldn't hear the sounds that she made. He felt the way she moved. The impatient panting of her breath, the rise and fall of her hips against his, the heat of her body against his erection.

Adam nudged her closer again and enjoyed the way they fit together. Oh, how he needed that feeling. Needed her against him.

Leaning up, he opened his mouth to pay the same kind of delicious attention to her other breast but found himself trapped by her hands. They framed his face and held him still as she plundered his mouth, her tongue sweeping deep against his while his hands continued their tender exploration of her body.

"Adam," she pulled back on a gasp as his hands dropped down and started to work on the button of her pants, "hurry."

She peppered kisses on his face until he pulled away as he succeeded in working her buttons free.

"How," he asked as her mouth closed over his earlobe, "your arms-"

"I may be curvy," she gave him a wink, "but I'm flexible." She leaned back and got to her feet, extending her hand to him. "Want to see just how flexible I am?"

Sitting there, already hard as a spike, his eyes passing over Blake's beautiful body, half bare and filling out her jeans like a goddess, he only had one choice.

The truth.

"Nothing could stop me."

He reached out and took her hand and when he was almost standing Adam reached out his other hand and grabbed her hip, pulling her flush against him.

Groaning, he slid his hand down to grasp her butt as he

held her tight and pressed his lips against her throat. He trailed a long hot kiss along her skin until he found the lobe of her ear with his teeth.

Blake gasped and he felt the muscles in her backside tense against his hand. "I was hoping we'd take this into the bedroom."

He lifted his head and met her eyes, seeing the hunger he felt reflected in hers. "Oh, yeah, we're taking this in there."

"Then why the delay?" She arched her back and he felt the tight points of her breasts push against him.

He swore under his breath, shaking his head. "You had to mention flexible."

She licked her lips and he almost came in his pants like a teenage boy eager for his first taste of oblivion. "Then let's test it out and make sure that I'm not a liar... just on the run."

"Yes, ma'am."

Oh, her eyes sparkled.

"Ma'am?"

"Don't argue, woman. I'm trying to agree with you."

"But then you called me-"

"Mine."

That stopped her on a dime and her eyes softened for a moment and lord help him, she leaned in and pressed a kiss to his lips.

It should have burned with all the lust surging through his veins, but he melted into her kiss and lost the last barrier between them.

He was lost... and found in her kiss.

It should have been impossible.

Having lost so much in his life. Half of his battalion and so many others along the way, he had to work to keep his heart open to his family.

His lifeline.

But now, holding Blake close, feeling her beautiful body

against his, and tasting the tender sweetness of her lips, he felt his heart swell and throb with life.

He was in love with Blake Lennox.

When she moved away, she looked down and saw his fingers hooked through one of the belt loops of her jeans.

He started walking, backwards at first, and then he turned, leading her behind him into his bedroom.

Fuck, he growled to himself, *their* bedroom.

As he neared the bed, he saw her lift an arm across her chest and he pulled her close with a shake of his head. "don't cover yourself, baby. I want to see you. All of you."

Setting her in place with the foot of the bed at her back he grasped the waist of her jeans and tugged.

They peeled off and he held them so she could step out, her hands delicately touching his shoulders. Already down on one knee, he went weak as she slipped her thumbs into the edge of her cream-colored panties, complete with a tiny bow centered beneath her belly button, and slipped them over the swell of her hips.

He followed her hands all the way to her knees and watched her lift one foot and then the other before dropping them at her feet.

From there, he followed her hands as they smoothed up her legs, and then her hips, giving him a tantalizing view of her body.

Before he'd made a conscious decision, he was on his feet, and his hands on her.

Setting her on the edge of his bed, he reached behind him, over his head, and pulled off his shirt. "Scoot up, baby." He lifted his chin toward the head of the bed. "I wanted to taste you first," his tongue passed over his lower lip as she inched back over his sheets.

"Fuck," he had to reach down and ease the pressure of his

pants against his cock, "I'm going to dream about this moment for the rest of my life, baby."

Her warm suntanned skin against the cinnamon brown of his sheets was better than anything he'd ever seen or imagined before.

As she found the center of the bed, she looked him over with hunger in her eyes and her thighs squeezed together around her hands.

"Adam, please."

As if he wasn't hard enough already, the needy sound of her voice cut him deep.

Made him ache deep in his soul.

Reaching into his pocket, he pulled out a condom wrapper. "One day," he told her, "we're not going to need these." He noticed the shock in her expression, but he didn't say anything more.

Placing the wrapper between his teeth at the corner of his mouth, he reached down and popped his button open.

He kept his eyes on Blake and saw that her eyes were on him.

When he took hold of the pull on his zipper, Blake propped herself up on an elbow. He pulled it down and her lips parted along with her knees.

And damn if her fingers didn't slip into the curls between her legs as he wrapped his hand around his cock.

"You're trying to kill me, Blake." The words were barely audible with his teeth closed around the wrapper

"I'm trying to get you to come over here."

Adam shoved his pants down, struggling with the briefs that had to slide off and not strangle his dick as he moved. He got one knee down on the bed and shook his pants off the other a second before he climbed on the bed and really, even if he hadn't, it wouldn't have mattered.

He wanted to get to her and he'd gladly spend the rest of

the night with his jeans tangled around his foot if she was tangled in his sheets.

Adam crawled up between her legs and dragged his gaze up along her leg and to the sight of her fingers stroking through her heat.

Tearing the wrapper open, Adam pulled the condom free and tossed the pieces to the side. "Do you have any idea how sexy you look?"

Hesitation clouded her eyes and her fingers slowed their movements.

"Don't, baby. Please don't stop."

Her gaze dipped down to the side and the flush in her cheeks wasn't just from desire. "I wasn't sure-"

"If you want to touch yourself, do it." His throat worked over the tight lump lodged inside of it. "What makes you feel good, looks damn good to me. I want to know what you like. If you want to show it to me, fuck yes."

He saw her curl her fingers between her folds and he fumbled the condom on the bed.

She lifted her sloe-eyes to him and he felt a drop of pre-cum fall onto his hand.

"You need help with that, Adam?"

He shook his head, but he didn't look down to find the condom. His searching fingers found it in seconds. "If you touch me now, I'm going to embarrass myself." Gritting his teeth together he tried to ignore how difficult it was to slide the condom over his erection. Necessary, but damn painful in the situation.

Once he had it on, he only had to focus on one thing. Making his girl happy.

Moving closer, until his knee bumped up against her thigh, he gave her a look. "Hand me a pillow, baby."

Her eyes widened a hint, but she reached back and

grabbed a pillow without questioning him. He tugged it out of her hand.

"I can't wait to get inside you, Blake. I'm going to make you lose your mind."

Breathless, she gave him a smile. "Do it. I want you so bad."

He dropped the pillow over his knees and reached under to lift her hips. She set her feet down on the bed and helped him, giving him the most amazing view of her body. She was perfection. Beyond her dark chocolate curls, he could see the glistening folds of her sex, and he was done waiting.

With the pillow under her hips and the dark depths of passion in her eyes, his heart was thundering in his chest. The need to love and protect her, body and soul, was more than instinct, it was a need like his next breath.

Rising halfway up on his knees, his cock in his hand, he leaned into her and felt the first pull of her body. As the tip sank into her body, he heard her soft, breathy sigh in his ears.

"More."

"You're a greedy woman, aren't you?"

She looked up at him and smiled. "With you?"

He couldn't help feeling his back teeth grinding against each other at the thought of any other man with her. "Of course."

"Yes." Blake lifted her arms and held out her hand to him. "Yes, Adam. With you, I want everything." She pulled her lower lip into her mouth and he saw her teeth bite down as her lip pulled free. "Fill me up."

How could he tell her no when that's all he wanted for the rest of his life? Leaning forward he caught her hands and pressed them back against the mattress as his cock pushed all the way inside of her body. When he bottomed out, he let out a groan and heard Blake answer him with one of her own.

Balls deep and hovering over her gorgeous face he felt as if he might be in the middle of a dream. "You feel so good."

She stretched beneath him, her breasts rising to trail her nipples across his skin. "You too."

When she wiggled under him the edges of his vision darkened. The friction of her body around his, the soft swell of her body cushioning him, every inch of contact was bliss.

"I can't make this slow." The admission killed him, but it was the plain truth.

"Good." Blake squeezed his hands and met his eyes with a level gaze. "Because I want you hard and fast, Adam. I need it. I need you." And if he wasn't already on the edge, she pushed him closer when she wrapped her legs around his middle and pulled him impossibly deeper. A soft laugh burst from her lips. "Yes, like that... deep, like that."

Could she be any more perfect?

He rose up higher on his knees and felt her legs ease up on their hold as he withdrew from her body almost to the tip of his cock before he pushed right back inside.

Adam felt her body stretch around him and once he was fully seated again, tightened like a hand, grasping at his length. "Just like that," her smile lit her up from inside and he repeated the motion, "yes."

Blake nodded and then shook her head as he withdrew again. "Don't leave me."

"Never, baby." He surged back inside of her body. "Never."

Over and over he sank into her body, slowing only to lift one of her legs and draw it up along his chest, pressing a kiss to the inside of her ankle before repeating it with her other leg and it was worth the momentary hesitation when he sank into her again and heard her throaty cry.

"Yes! Oh god, yes!"

He felt it. Felt the eager pull of her inner walls against his cock. Felt the tightening of her muscles as he continued to move within her again and again. And her voice, a long string of words and hungry sounds pouring from her lips, told him he was close, so deliciously close to giving her the kind of pleasure she deserved.

"Come for me, baby." He ground himself against her at the end of each thrust and saw her reach her hands up to grasp the sheets above her head. Watching her head tip back and turn side to side as she struggled to catch her breath made him feel like a king, a conquering hero. "A little farther, Blake. Hold me tight."

Adam sucked in a breath as her body gripped him, pulling at him with each successive thrust.

"So. Damn. Close." Her hips lifted from the pillow and he almost fell over her, but he held on.

"More," she panted and his hungry eyes saw the way her breasts shook, "just a little more!"

And he gave it to her.

The sheets pulled free of the mattress and her hands pulled them close about her head. Her eyes were wide open but she couldn't seem to focus them on his face, but what mattered the most was the way she seemed to float in his arms.

She came apart and her body caressed him like a velvet glove, her muscles contracting along his cock in waves. She pulled his orgasm from him, sending electricity arcing through his spine as he emptied himself inside of her.

And when he felt the last shivers of his orgasm echoing through his body, he gathered her close, held her gently against him as he found enough of his blankets to cover her.

Blake pressed a kiss to his shoulder and then to his chest as she settled her hand over his heart.

Adam wrapped his hand around her to stroke the curve of her hip.

"Adam?"

He managed to make his throat work to answer her back. "Yeah, baby?"

Her sigh feathered across his heated skin. "Thank you."

He had to turn her words over and over in his head before he understood them. "Why?"

"Because..." She snuggled in against his side and started to fall asleep.

"Babe?" He didn't want to nudge her or anything like that, but he wanted to know the answer. "Why?"

"Because," she yawned, "I finally feel safe."

And then she fell asleep.

CHAPTER 13

ROBERT CLIMBED out of his car and looked around at what looked to be the main cross streets of Eagle Rock, Montana and ended up squinting to avoid the early morning sunlight. "What a backwater piece of-"

"Well, hello there, stranger!"

Turning, he found an old man sizing him up from the sidewalk. The man's cowboy hat was pushed so far back on his head that his receding hairline was just visible in the afternoon sun.

"You moving in or through?"

Robert stared at the old man, hoping he'd get the point and walk on.

"Well, either way, I should welcome you to town." He looked down at the beagle on a leash beside him. "Don't mind the dog," he chuckled, "he ain't one to bite more than once a decade."

Nodding, Robert bit back a few choice words for the talkative old man.

"If you're hungry. There's a diner just across the street and a bit. Don't forget to go to the Moose if you've a taste for something more than coffee or pop later in the day. You here to sightsee?"

His shoulders sagged a bit, silence wasn't working. "Just here to stretch my legs and fill up on gas and food."

Nodding his satisfaction, the older man gave the leash a tug. "Well, you better get on down to the diner. Seats fill up around this time of day."

With a tip of his chin, the old man continued down the sidewalk and Robert swore under his breath. "The last thing I need are a bunch of nosey people getting in my way."

Closing the driver's door, Robert moved around the hood and stepped up on the sidewalk to stand under a bright colored awning. He needed some time to take a look around and the awning gave him some shade to work with and a tree nearby gave him even more shadows and cover.

He wasn't expecting there to be much of a problem finding the girl. There couldn't be more than a hundred people living in and around the main part of town. A couple hundred in the outer lying areas.

It wasn't going to be possible to snoop around Sadie Patterson's house. The whole ranch was likely a security nightmare, for him. Still, if the people in town were as friendly as the old man was, he was going to be back on the road by nightfall with Blake Lennox tied up in his trunk.

His stomach rumbled and he looked across the street for the diner the man was talking about it. He found it easy enough. There were, what, a half dozen businesses on the other side of the street.

The diner was near the center. Even though the town wasn't anything to speak of, he bet it would be a step up from the usual greasy spoon if he was lucky. It would be easy enough to get information out of a waitress. They were always looking for ways to get a better tip and women would notice a new girl in town. No one liked competition even in a Podunk town like this one.

Clicking the lock on his key fob, Robert stepped out into the street and crossed without any danger. There wasn't even one single hayseed cowboy on a horse trotting down main street. So much for that quaint country town experience reporters talked about when they mentioned Sadie.

He'd made it up onto the curb when the door to the diner swung open and a young woman ran out with a couple of brown paper bags in her arms. She saw him and looked up in surprise. "Oh, sorry. In a rush." And yes, she was. She moved off down the sidewalk in her ugly sneakers, but the calves visible between the ankle socks and the blue pastel waitress uniform were worth a second look.

Come to think about it, her ass was decent, and the face he'd seen in passing was pretty.

The diner wasn't going anywhere. Turning on his heel he started to walk in her direction but kept his strides easy and casual. He wasn't there to attract attention.

She had a big brown paper bag tucked up under her arm, but she still managed to keep her steps quick and purposeful.

Cutting through a parking lot, she passed by a car and disappeared around a corner.

Robert looked up at the sign. Masterson Mechanics.

His gaze dropped down to the car in the parking lot. Pulling his phone from his pocket he laid his thumb on the face of the phone and unlocked it and found the picture he took of the old woman's scrapbook. The same crappy paint-job on the VW Bug. Same old crooked rear fender.

It couldn't be this easy. The car limping into the same town that Sadie Patterson lived in? Perfect.

He started a call and ground his back teeth until the line picked up.

"Found the car. I'll have the girl soon. Have Nolan head

toward my location. I may need a little help. No, I'm sure I can handle it, but this town is tiny. If we want to get her out of town quietly, it will probably take the two of us."

He listened as Seth threatened him, but it all sounded like *blah blah blah*, because while Robert might be paid muscle, he wasn't as stupid as Seth thought he was. He was watching out for himself too. He'd seen Seth burn others when they'd outlived their usefulness. Now, he was going to get Blake Lennox under his control and then he was going to make sure he had control of the situation. It was time to grab a little power for himself.

Just in time, he saw the waitress come back into view. Robert switched his hold on the phone and stared at it like he was intent on reading something on the screen.

Humming to herself, the waitress moved passed him and walked back into the diner.

Taking a step to the side, Robert cast a side-long glance up the side of the building, intent on getting a good look at the structure, but movement in an upstairs window drew his attention.

The curtain bunched and fell back down into place.

Someone was upstairs.

Dropping his focus down to the ground floor he saw a man moving under a four-door sedan up on a lift. He was wearing an old-style coverall, but the man wasn't the kind of pot-bellied, beer guzzling gomer he expected. Nope. The way the man moved, he had training in something more than oil changes.

There was muscle that came from hard work and dedicated training.

If Seth thought she was alone in the world, he was wrong, and she'd likely already enlisted Sadie's help.

If that was true, this was going to be even more difficult. Robert had his own training, but he'd learned his own limits the hard way. None of them had a thing to do with women.

He'd do what he had to.

And when it was done, Seth would realize he was more than just muscle. He deserved his own measure of power.

Seth would learn.

They all would.

BLAKE SAT down at the table and looked at the brown bags that Annalise had left with her. She was starving but it took a moment for her to open the bags and start to unpack the plates that she'd brought. Apparently, Adam had flagged his sister down on her way to work and asked her to bring food over for breakfast.

Somehow, Annalise had gotten the impression that Blake might be tired and hungry.

Well, his sister had used words with more color and the look in her eyes had told Blake that she knew exactly why Blake was dead tired and a little tender.

Worse than the walk of shame, Blake had to deal with the fact that her boyfriend had basically told his sister that they'd spent all night long… doing things.

Yeah, she couldn't even think it, let alone say it, but it still made her blush. All over.

And boyfriend?

Where had that thought come from?

Ugh.

Blake laid her forehead down on the table and squeezed her eyes shut. What was she doing?

Her morning sip of whine gave way to her hunger as the scent of maple syrup reached her nose.

Popping the top off one box she saw four thick slices of

soft, pillowy French toast. "Oh, thank heavens!" Setting aside the little container of butter, she quickly cut up the triangles of doughy battered goodness and poured every single drop of maple syrup over her breakfast.

And that was what she focused on for a few minutes, but soon enough Blake's mind found its way back into the same cycle of worry. She just couldn't escape the feeling that things were about to change. It felt like the very ground beneath her feet was shifting by millimeters.

Maybe it was just that she was used to the way things were in Los Angeles and here in Montana everything seemed so different.

Easier.

Slower.

But there was no ignoring the rising tide of unease that was welling up inside of her.

This, she knew, could all end.

Time with Adam. Enjoying his gentle manner and the passion of his kisses was a heady experience.

It was all too easy to forget the world outside when he was holding her against his body. His muscles against the softer curves of her breasts, her thighs, created a delicious friction.

She had never enjoyed sex much, but just the touch of his hand against her body, even through her clothing, made her quake and shiver.

And he never pushed.

Never made a move that might scare her.

It was all perfect.

Maybe too perfect.

NO.

She shook her head and popped the last bit of syrup-covered toast into her mouth.

Don't look the gift horse in the mouth. Enjoy the

moments. This was what she had never even allowed herself to hope for, so what was the harm in enjoying it. Taking happiness securely in both hands because she knew sooner or later she would have to go back and face... whoever she had to because Zoe had been a good friend to her and to return the favor she would have to stand up to Seth and possibly whoever he owned in the LAPD and make them take a second look at her death.

She knew, deep down inside, that Zoe hadn't taken her own life. Blake had been through the exact same thing, but no one had stopped it for Blake. Seth had touched her all over and crawled into her head just as deep as he had been inside of her body.

So, Zoe wouldn't have done that to herself.

Right?

Dropping her fork onto the nearly empty take-out container, Blake stared down at the hands she'd dropped into her lap. "Think, Blake, think!"

How was she going to make this happen when everyone else seemed to believe that Zoe had taken her own life?

How was she going to make it back to Los Angeles and get the memory card from its hiding place without drawing unwanted attention to Sadie's family and Adam's as well?

The more she thought about it, the more she realized that she was out of her league. That was probably the reason why her career had been one seemingly endless list of quirky, best friend roles instead of the bigger role she had as 'Sharp-shooter Sally.'

Blake shook her head. Even that was kind of laughable by Hollywood standards.

Just how was she supposed to pull this off without dragging innocent people in?

Standing up, she picked up her take-out box and headed over to the trash can. Dumping it in she couldn't help but feel like the action mimicked the feelings inside of her, all going down in the dumps.

"Pathetic," she groused at herself as she decided what to do next in her pretty little prison of her own making.

~

SOMETHING WAS GNAWING at the back of his mind.

And no, it wasn't Annalise's overt hinting that she had their mother's engagement ring in her jewelry box.

There was something dark in the back of his head, like someone waiting in the shadows to take Blake away from him.

If he thought that falling in love might purge his dark thoughts and nightmares, he would be wrong.

Falling in love with Blake Lennox had only brought home even more fear and worry. What if someone did take her away? What if she went back to Los Angeles and realized that what they'd shared had been little more than a diversion from her life?

Would he be able to convince her it wasn't?

Should he even try?

"Damn it!" Adam stared down at the blood streaming from his finger. He'd taken his mind off his work and now he was paying the price.

Heading to the sink at the side of the shop he looked out the window and his gaze settled on Blake's car. Hissing with pain as the water coursed over his wound he swore under his breath. "I've got to move that thing in here and cover it up."

Blake said she'd left her car behind with the older woman. If they managed to track Blake that far, would they be able to find the Bug? "It's not like they came with GPS tracking back then. So maybe we're okay."

"Well, if you're talking to yourself, I should get you an

appointment with a therapist, or maybe you're losing your mind over Blake."

Adam turned to look at Hank and saw the other man grinning at him with a knowing look.

"Looks like you've fallen like the rest of us."

"I'm sorry, I don't know what you're-"

"In love, Adam." Hank's tone didn't leave room for an argument. "You've fallen for her."

Reaching out for the first aid kit attached to the wall, Adam popped open the cover and started to root around for the right supplies.

Hank pushed his hand out of the way. "Let me help you or you're going to bleed all over."

"Okay, so I fell for her." Adam stepped away and grabbed a clean cloth to wipe away the water and excess blood. "But it's not going to work out. *We're* not going to work out." Saying the words only made them feel more real.

Busy setting up the necessary supplies on the clean space beside the sink, Hank didn't bother to say a word. Adam felt like he was just waiting for something. And normally, he wasn't a man who just said something to fill a void, but things weren't normal anymore.

"Just because you and Sadie worked out-"

"Swede and my sister, Allie." Hank ripped opened a wrap-around finger bandage made to work over a knuckle. "And then Tate and Mia."

Adam stared at him as Hank sprayed some antiseptic on the cut. "Okay, okay, so a few couples-"

"Duke and Angel," Hank paused to fold the arms of the bandage down, "and don't forget Taz and Hannah."

"Okay!" Adam hung his head and struggled not to say the thoughts that were really on the tip of his tongue. "I get the point, but this is different, Hank."

Balling up the rubbish, Hank tossed it in the trash can

nearby. "Right. We've all been there, Adam. We've all faced crazy obstacles and we've all walked through fire for love. The question isn't 'if' it would work out for you and Blake. The question is are you willing to fight for it? What Blake is going through right now can't be easy. I know from talking to Sadie that after she moved here Blake and Zoe really leaned on each other. And Blake doesn't like dragging people into her troubles. That's probably why she didn't share everything that happened to her.

"Are you ready to push past that kind of a barrier?"

Adam stared at the bandage on his finger and then looked up at his friend. "I don't know. When Annalise was pregnant, I promised myself that I would be there for my sister and her baby, and what I feel for Blake is amazing. Crazy and amazing. I never expected to find someone that makes me feel the way she does… but I'm not sure she would even want me to try. I know that I love her and that's not going to go away."

His chin dropped down to his chest and he felt his heart pounding almost violently inside of his ribs.

"I'd rather focus on something I can do."

Hank's expression was pretty telling, but he added words to it. "And that would be?"

"Keeping her safe from that maniac Seth Coleman. So, tell me what else I can do to help?"

"Right now?" Hank blew out a breath. "Keep her here and safe. I have one of my new men on a plane to Hollywood. Paxton Fullerton has an old military connection to a detective with the LAPD. He thinks he can get through that way and get us either some information to fix this or maybe find another way to solve this."

There was an edge to Hank's voice that Adam almost didn't recognize.

"Coleman's a predator. Praying on dreams and women

too afraid to speak up for themselves. We have to find a way to stop this."

"That," Adam nodded, "I can totally agree on. I just wish we could keep Blake out of this. Maybe I can find out where she hid the memory card and retrieve it, turn it into the LAPD myself. The last thing I want to do is let her get within a thousand miles of Seth Coleman."

Hank agreed. "That might not be possible, but I like the way you think, Adam. I'm just sorry I couldn't convince you to work with us. You would be a formidable guard with your history."

Adam couldn't help the look he directed up toward his apartment. All his thoughts kept drifting back to Blake.

"Honestly, Hank… it's not my history I'm concerned with, so much as my future."

CHAPTER 14

"Okay, so I fell for her. But it's not going to work out. We're not going to work out."

Blake had been half a step away from the door when she'd heard Adam's words to Hank and that had stopped her in place sending her right back upstairs.

Wow.

Talk about a slap in the face!

No, she couldn't really blame Adam. He thought he'd fallen for her. Well, she'd fallen right back, but now there wasn't any reason to tell him. Not when he'd shut the door.

Pushing open the closet door she stared at the handful of outfits dangling from hangers before her, hanging her head. She had to figure something out and quick. The more she leaned on Adam, the more she felt like an albatross around his neck.

The last thing she wanted him to do is be relieved when she finally left. She wanted him to remember her with a smile and maybe even a few 'what ifs' and 'could've beens.' That would be all she would have too.

Taking out the most nondescript thing that Annalise had picked out for her, she pulled open the top drawer of Adam's dresser and picked out a pair of underwear from the stash that had arrived in the mail. She ignored Adam's socks and boxer-briefs; it would be too easy to think of how perfect they looked in the same drawer.

With a resolute nod, she closed the top drawer and brought her things into the bathroom. She would shower and then head over to the diner. If she was lucky, she could crawl into one of the back booths and hide out for a bit. There would be enough folks there that she could go unnoticed in the rush and people watching was always a favorite hobby. She could let her mind wander and hopefully figure out some kind of actual plan to get real justice for Zoe and herself out of this horrible, stupid mess.

Not to mention the added bonus, the physical distance from Adam would help too. It was impossible to do much when every room of his apartment reminded her of him. And just how much she'd fallen for him even before he'd shown her that she was desirable just as she was.

No matter what else, she knew he hadn't faked that between them. That she would hold in her heart forever.

Setting down her clothes beside the sink she turned on the shower.

ADAM TIPPED his gaze up toward the ceiling. The pipes in the building were great, but he could still hear the water coursing through them. Smiling, he thought of Blake in the shower.

He would have loved to join her, but one look at the water coursing over her body and he'd forget what he'd been tasked with, protecting her. Something he'd lost sight of in the need to find his comfort in her embrace. What people and their small-mindedness had done to her spirit was criminal. If they couldn't see how beautiful she is they should keep their thoughts to themselves.

And he really needed to get his head on straight. His first responsibility was to make sure that Seth Coleman didn't touch Blake's life any more than he already had.

After that, well, he'd figure out what to do next when next came.

Picking up his wrench, he went right back to work.

That, he could handle.

No one could ever accuse her of being ready for American Ninja or even American Gladiators, although they had a few girls with curves on their show. Okay, so their curves were mostly solid muscle, but curves.

Yep, she was also delusional when she stressed.

That's normal, right?

Still, she made it to the bottom of the outside stairs and around the back of the building without Adam seeing her. It helped that he was up to his elbows in foreign car parts.

Cutting through a little alleyway that was just bigger than the width of her hips, she found her way to the front of the diner. Pulling the hood of her hoodie back and away from her face she walked purposefully through the room as if she had been there a thousand times before.

True to form, folks treated her like she was invisible and what normally drove her nuts had become a mark in the plus column for once.

She saw Annalise near a booth at the back of the room.

She could only see part of her face, but she could tell her new friend anywhere, there was just something singular about Adam's sister.

With a smile she walked up to Annalise and popped around front to catch her attention. "Hey, sorry to bother, but-"

She stopped talking as soon as she saw the man sitting in the booth.

"Robert." That's right. While she didn't really know much about Seth's right hand security stooge, she knew his name and enough about him to realize that she was in deep trouble.

Even worse, Annalise was in danger.

And that wasn't an overactive imagination or blowing things out of proportion. There was a gun in the shoulder holster that Robert always wore and the way he had his jacket open at the moment, the handgrip of his pistol was a stark contrast to the faded chambray shirt he was wearing.

"Hello, Blake. How lucky to see you here."

She nodded, slowly, unwilling to make any sudden movements around the security goon. "You must have stepped in a big pile of something."

He smiled. "You mean like you did?"

She heard the smug tone in his voice and it sliced through her making it difficult to speak, but she had to say something to buy them time. "Well, at least my luck is holding, right?" She licked at her lips and found them suddenly dry. "Is Seth here in Eagle Rock?"

Robert adjusted the hold he had on Annalise's arm and Blake saw her friend wince in pain. "You think he'd come here?" Shaking his head, Robert gave Annalise a measuring look. "Can you believe how stupid she is?"

Blake saw Annalise's jaw tense a heartbeat before she tried to open her mouth and speak. She could tell by the look in her friend's eyes that it wasn't a good idea to let this go on.

"I didn't think so. I just thought I'd ask. This would be like his own personal hell, right?"

That got a smile from him. "I doubt we could score him coke all the way out here, and I doubt there's discreet service for girls either. He'd rather die than set foot in this town."

Nodding slowly, Blake reached out to touch Annalise in comfort, but Robert saw the gesture first. "Don't do that," he warned her, "unless you're trying to get your friend killed."

Lifting her hand slowly away from Annalise, Blake gave him a look that said she understood what he was saying, and then she told him, "Okay then. You're the boss."

"And the Boss is fucking hungry. So," he grinned up at Annalise, "you're going to get me a burger with everything, a pile of fries, and coffee. And make no mistake, I'm watching you, so no passing notes or side conversations. Understand?"

Annalise stood completely quiet and still for a moment, long enough to grate on Robert's nerves.

"Or I could shoot you dead right here and drag your friend out to the car in a heartbeat."

"There's one thing you forget about places 'all the way out here.'"

"Oh?" He smiled, but the curve of his lips looked more like a coiling snake than a man. "And just what is that?"

Annalise's eyes flared with hope for a moment. "This is Montana. There's more cowboys and hunters here than you can literally shake a stick at. If you draw that gun in here, there is no guarantee that you'll make it out that door."

Robert turned a little on the bench seat and scanned the diner patrons. Blake watched him assess each and every person in the room.

"Okay," he spoke to no one in particular, "then this is how we're going to play it. Blake with her ridiculous new haircut is going to sit down and we'll wait for you to bring me my food. When I'm done eating, we're all going to take a walk out to my car. And then I'm going to decide what we do from there."

Blake couldn't keep quiet. "You can't hurt her, Robert. I'll do whatever you want but you need to leave her here."

He leaned forward on the table and stared at her. "I'm sorry, but when did you get to be in charge?"

"She's a local," Blake argued with a smile trying to keep her expression light enough that no one else would key into the tension she was feeling. It wouldn't do any of them good for someone to get curious. "If you put her in a car and take her out of town, they'll notice."

Robert at least gave it some thought. "We'll see, but I'm hungry and I don't think for shit on an empty stomach."

Annalise looked at him with a nod. "I'll bring something over for both of you to eat."

Trying to keep her expression staid, Blake let out a breath. She didn't want to say anything to upset the gunman.

He had no such worries. "Oh, don't bother bringing something for Blake. Her fat ass could use a few less calories. Now hurry up."

Blake gave her friend an easy smile. "Please, Annalise, do as he says."

When she walked away, Blake sank back against the booth and turned to look at Robert. "How did you find me?"

He gave her a look that made her blood run cold. "I've had to track you all over the western half of the country and if you think you're not going to pay for that, you're stupider than Seth says you are."

"I just wanted to know. That's all."

"Found your phone. Found your car."

Blake felt all the blood drain from her face. "My car."

"Yes, your car." His eyes sharpened, focusing on her face.

"That little old lady was so sweet. When I told her how worried I was about you and how much I wanted you home so I could help take care of our baby, she was so excited she wanted to bake a damn cake. So, I let her start up that oven."

Blake's stomach turned over. "No."

"And when she bent over to stick that damn toothpick in to see if it was done-"

"Please. No." Her throat burned with acid and she could almost taste the bile climbing up onto the back of her tongue. "Please tell me you-"

"Well, she must have waxed her floors," he smiled, "because she slipped and her head hit that damn oven door with a smack so loud-"

"Oh please no."

"I can still hear the *crack* in my ears now."

Blake had to swallow back the rush of bile that threatened to make her empty her stomach right then and there. She knew she couldn't do it. Knew how much danger that Annalise and the rest of the people in the diner were in.

"You can't really blame me for this, Blake." He sounded perfectly reasonable in his tone. "I couldn't exactly leave her to tell tales, could I?"

The world around her dimmed, the sounds of the diner drowned under the sounds of blood rushing through her ears, and there was a taste that erased the acidic crawl of bile on her tongue. Blood.

WHEN JACK MORGAN pushed through the door into the workroom, Adam gave him an odd look. "Hey, Jack, long time-"

"Son, you know I think the world of your sister, but is there any chance she can come back and finish out her shift? We got some kind of tour group that showed up and we were already strapped when she left to come and help her friend pack. I didn't even know you had someone staying with you, but I've got a full house and-"

"Hold on!" He knew that he'd added a little too much force behind his words when the older man drew up and nailed Adam with a look that said he'd stepped over the line. "Annalise left with who?"

With a huff, Jack answered again. "Her friend. Short curly hair, kinda big in the hips. You know her, right?"

Adam let the slight go, he had bigger issues at the moment.

"Yeah, I do. Anyway. Thanks for letting me know. As soon as I talk to Annalise, I'll let her know."

Dropping everything, Adam turned around and headed inside.

Jack called after him. "That's it? As soon as you talk to her? Don't you know where she is?"

Adam only heard the last bit of the older man's outrage as he hustled up the stairs almost three at a time.

When he turned the knob, he called out loud enough to be heard inside. "Annalise? Blake?"

He reached into his pocket and realized that he'd left the keys on his workbench downstairs.

Letting out a shuddering breath, he banged on the door again. "Blake? Damn it! Are you in there?" His heart squeezed in his chest and he mumbled under his breath. "Please, baby, answer the damn door."

When the apartment remained silent, he lost any semblance of patience. Stepping back, he kicked the door open, blowing it inward on its hinges.

The room was still.

Cold.

Without even going into the bedroom he knew that Blake was gone.

And he had a sinking feeling that Annalise was too.

Stepping over to the kitchen counter he picked up the phone and dialed Hank.

When the phone call picked up he didn't even wait for a greeting.

"I need your help."

WHEN HANK ARRIVED, he walked straight through the door since it was still hanging off its hinges. Sadie was only a half-step behind him. "What happened?"

Adam sighed. "From everything I can figure out. Blake went to see Annalise at the diner. Jack told me that Annalise left with Blake to help her pack."

Sadie and Hank shared a look.

Hank looked back at Adam. "Who else was there?"

Shaking his head, Adam felt as if a knife was twisting in his chest. "A man. Jack didn't get a good look, just that he was tall and looked out of place. He thought he was with Blake."

"And your sister?"

He knew the question was coming and it still killed him to think the words let alone say them.

"Jack said she didn't come back that's why he came to see me. I called her sitter and Ada is fine and with them, but they haven't heard from her either."

Hank shook his head and Sadie curled into his side. "Someone came into our town and took them."

Adam looked up at him with anguish in his eyes and radiating through his chest. "Yeah."

Reaching into his coat, Hank pulled out his phone. "We'll get them back."

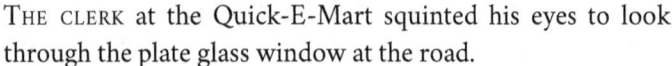

THE CLERK at the Quick-E-Mart squinted his eyes to look through the plate glass window at the road.

"Who the hell is that?"

There was someone walking down the road toward the store.

That was crazy. They were at least ten miles from the nearest town.

"Uh, Mister Miles!"

It took a moment for the older man to make his way out of the storeroom.

"Mister Miles, look!"

The store owner moved to the front windows and stared out along the road. "What is she doing out there?" There were only a few steps to the front door, but he kept pausing and muttering under his breath. "Crazy fools."

"I dunno, Mister Miles. She looks like she's in trouble."

Nodding, the owner gestured at the door. "Go and help her in. We'll see what kind of help she needs."

On any other day the clerk would have grumbled under his breath. Old Mister Miles made him do more than his fair share of work, but in this case, he wanted to help.

Jogging down the road he came up on the woman and stopped short when she reared back, shock apparent in her eyes and posture. "Hey, hey," he smiled and held his hands out at his sides. "I'm not going to hurt you. I just want to help."

She gasped in a breath and nodded. "I need a phone."

"Okay," he held out his hand, "can I help you the rest of the way. You can call from inside the store?"

Reaching out, she grasped his hand as if it was a lifeline. "Yes… thank you."

He held her hand and wrapped the other arm around her

as they moved toward the store, faster than she had been moving before.

"What- what happened to you?"

"Not me." Shaking her head, she struggled forward faster still. "My friend. They took my friend. I need to tell my brother."

CHAPTER 15

WAITING HAD NEVER BEEN Adam's strong suit. Never.

Even When Annalise was in labor, he'd been the one pacing in the room and then outside the room when his sister had all but evicted him from her room. In the time since he'd received a call from his sister at some roadside mini mart, he'd gone through the whole gamut of emotions.

Relief that he knew his sister was going to be on her way home. Hope that Blake was still alive the last time that Annalise saw her. If they were just trying to keep Blake from being able to tell her story then they would have just... they could have just...

But they were taking her somewhere.

And it wasn't going to be anywhere near. At least not their final destination. Hank had someone running down flights out of nearby airports and his contact in Los Angeles was working with his police contact to see what kind of activity was happening at Megalodon Studios and more specifically what Seth Coleman was up to.

All the while that was happening, Adam felt like he was treading water and sinking deeper and deeper into despair and worry. Until he had both Annalise and Blake home he wasn't going to rest.

Home.

He needed Blake to come back home.

To him.

His cell rang and he pulled it out of his back pocket, answering it on the first ring. "Hank?"

Hank's tone was even over the line. "Security cameras confirm that they left out of Bozeman on a private jet. No one's even trying to hide it. They must be pretty confident at this point."

"They have a jump on me. That's all they have." He was already on his feet, so it only took a few second for him to get to the closet on the far side of the room and slide open the door.

"They have a jump on us," the other man reminded him. "How do you want to handle this, Adam?"

He had a feeling that the smile on his face was more feral than anything else. Adam could feel the tight stretch of his lips as he reached into the recesses of the closet and keyed in the passcode for his safe. "Go in, get her back."

Hank murmured an agreement on the other end of the call.

Adam continued with his plan. "Burn it to the ground so he can't do this again to anyone else."

There was a silence on the other end and then a slow hum of sound. "Maybe something a little less destructive for the second half of the mission would probably be better."

Adam wasn't anywhere near placated. "I can make it look like an accident."

Hank managed to smother most of his laugh, but Adam could still hear a little snort like sound on the other end. "You spend all of this time turning me down for a job and now you want to go full Rambo on this guy."

Adam's heart constricted painfully in his chest. "I want her back, Hank. I want her here, in my arms. In my bed. If he's touched her again, you're going to have to make a decision, Hank."

The silence on the other end was sharp like the edge of a bayonet poised to slide right through the ribs and into someone's lungs or heart.

"You're going to let me take him apart until there's nothing left but a stake through his black heart, or you're going to have to pull me off of him and get hurt in the process."

"I know where you are in your head, Adam, but you know without me having to say a word, that Blake wouldn't want you to put yourself in jeopardy like that."

Adam slipped his arm through the cross-body strap of his guncase and set the weight against his back before picking up his go bag laying on the floor like it had been waiting for him.

And maybe it had.

He was crossing the room to the door when Hank's voice reached through the line. "I'll have a few hours to try to get your head on straight," he sighed. "We'll be on the road in minutes and we'll pick you up. By the time we get to Bozeman they'll have a jet waiting for us."

Adam nodded. Hank knew him well enough to know his answer. "I'll be waiting out front."

On his way down the outside stairs, his phone rang again and he answered it with a curt command.

"Adam," Annalise's voice was only a tad higher than normal, "I just spoke to Sadie. She's invited me out to the ranch with Ada. We'll let the kids play together while we wait for news."

He didn't know what to say to that.

"You're going to get her and bring her back, aren't you?"

"I'm going to find her and I'm going to do everything I can to help her, but I'm not sure she's going to want to come back."

He heard his sister muttering under her breath. "You listen to me, dork."

Those were fighting words in their family. She was trying to get a rise out of him. If only she knew what it was taking for him to just try to hold himself together.

"She went with them for me, Adam. She went with them for Ada. I think she had another idea about what to do, but whatever it was, it wasn't this. Blake didn't *want* to go like that."

"I can't think about that. I have to concentrate on one thing. I have to make sure she's safe. Once that's done… it's up to her."

Annalise groaned and he heard the frustration in her voice. "Don't be so stubborn that you talk yourself out of going for what you want. For who you want."

"*'Lise*… I have to go, okay? I have to go."

"Fine." He could almost see her shaking her head at him. "Just don't be stupid."

He couldn't help but laugh at that. "I love you, too."

When the crew lowered the steps to the jet, Blake knew what she was going to do… everything in her power not to piss these men off. There was a time to be a boss and mouth off but this was not that time.

The airstrip was a private one and based on the care that the facility used to maintain their buildings it wasn't a well-used one. Looking around at the buildings closer to the fence she hoped that they would keep moving. The windows that were still intact were covered with grime and more than one door gaped open along some edge of the frame.

Nolan shoved her down the stairs and it took everything she had not to fall on her face. Blake was going to be forever thankful that she'd worn the sneakers that Annalise had picked up for her. At least her feet weren't going to hurt as much. Right?

Robert grabbed a hold of her arm and pulled her toward the fence line.

She turned her head back to see if any of the crew members were looking in her direction.

Maybe, just maybe, if one of them cared enough to look, she might have a chance.

The stairs were almost up when she looked and the only glimpse she caught of the crew was a hand and an elbow as the top part of the door was pulled down and snapped into place.

When they rounded the corner of the nearest building, she felt a little flare of hope burning inside of her. It was one of the heavily tinted black SUVs that practically littered the highways and freeways of California. Still, it meant more time and with that time, came a chance.

A chance that she might survive this.

The back door was thrown open from the inside of the vehicle and one of her new worst friends pushed her closer.

Yes, she wanted to tell them, she got it. Get in the car.

She was halfway up into the vehicle when someone smacked her backside.

Blake gasped in shock as the two men behind her laughed it up.

"Looks like you changed your style," he scoffed, "now we can see your fat ass."

Biting back the tears, Blake moved in toward the middle of the seat and reached for the seatbelt. She ignored their mocking comments as she sat still and tried to make herself invisible.

Time was what she needed.

If she had to take a few verbal slings and arrows, she'd do it gladly.

There was one thought that kept cycling through her head over and over and it was that Adam would find her.

Sure, he didn't want to be with her, but he had promised to help her.

And he was a man who did what he promised. She just had to hold on to that belief that he would help her through this and then she would walk away.

She would give him the gift of her absence, but he would always be with her in her heart. That would never change.

ADAM WAS the first one out of the vehicle and onto the tarmac, the others not far behind him. He barely turned his chin over his shoulder to speak as he walked. "You said this Paxton guy is already on the ground?"

"He's there and we'll have LAPD support if we have the time."

Hank's words tumbled through his head and almost made him stumble over the thoughts in Adam's head.

"I just want to find her and get her safe. If I have to do this all on my own. It will be done."

"Thank goodness you won't have to do that." Swede was the last one to climb into the jet and he looked around. "This is pretty fancy. Who got this for us?"

Hank waited for Taz to sit down before answering. "A friend of mine."

"A friend, huh?" Duke moved his bag aside with his foot

so that Tate could pass and sit down on another bench seat. "Someone we know?"

Tate gave Duke's boot a kick as he stretched out. "If we did, I think Hank would have just said his name."

Adam watched Hank sit back and let out a breath.

"*She* has several different codenames, but a few of us call her Wendy."

"Wendy?" Swede turned to look at Hank with an odd expression. "A few of 'us'?"

Tate chimed in. "Sounds like there's a story behind this 'Wendy' of yours."

Duke stretched out his legs and nodded. "Is there a Peter Pan too?"

"Peter?" The odd expression on Hank's face had nothing to do with the sudden tip of the plane on lift off from the small airstrip in Bozeman. "Yes, actually, but Wendy's the one in charge of the Lost Boys."

Swede cast a look around the group. "Then there's definitely a story."

"I could tell you all, but I'd have to kill you." Hank's expression didn't have a lick of humor in it. "Just know that if you meet Wendy it'll be on the other side of hell as you're coming home. She would tell you herself that you should count yourselves lucky if you *never* have to meet her.

"Still, she has a few nice toys at her disposal, including this jet. We'll arrive in California faster than other jets by about an hour. It won't make up for all the time we lost, but it will give us an advantage."

Adam flexed his hands into fists and let out a pent-up breath.

"I'll take any advantage we can get at this point."

Taz gave him a steady look. "We've got your back, Adam. We've got Blake's too."

Biting the inside of his cheek, Adam managed a few

words. "Thank you. All of you." He could feel everyone's eyes on him, offering their silent support. "We're going to get her back."

IT PROBABLY SHOULD HAVE SURPRISED her when the studio limo pulled up in the shadow of Stage Eight. Of course, they would bring her here. They'd gone through the trouble of bringing Zoe to the sound stage and she knew now that those rumors... that's exactly what they had been... had been a part of the plot to distance Seth from Zoe's death.

Washington DC had nothing on the Publicity Arm of Megalodon studios.

Need a fake story circulated? Check

Want to shape public perception? Check

So here she was at the same sound stage were Peggy Lindley's death had been attributed to the work of a vengeful ghost so many years before.

Zoe Rogers had been its most recent victim if you listened to the whispers.

And it seemed that there were plans to add her to the ever-growing list.

Would her end be gruesome enough to make it on one of the Hollywood Scandal tours that over-charged tourists for a couple of hours in a hot and crowded bus?

One of the men walking ahead of her turned on the flash-light in his phone to look around the immediate area.

Classy.

The center of the old warehouse had been cleaned up. She could see enough of her surroundings thanks to the moonlight sneaking in through some broken glass in the window high above the warehouse floor.

The stage was one of the original ten that were

constructed as part of the studio's beginnings and had office spaces along one wall, complete with a catwalk that lead to the old rigging cages high above the floor.

All together it wasn't as terrifying as if they'd dragged her out into the canyon, or the scrub brush on the top of one of the mountains.

Yep. Morose.

A single bulb clicked on a few feet away from the ladder in the center of the floor. An old ghost light with a bulb that flared and flickered as if it was almost more afraid of the dark than anything else.

A figure moved near the edge of the darkness and Blake suddenly realized what the light was afraid of.

"Hello, Blake." The way Seth said her name, a few droplets of spit caught the light and sparkled at the edge of the darkness. "So kind of you to join us."

"Us?" The question wasn't planned, just something she blurted out. She looked around the tight illuminated area and saw that Robert and Nolan had been joined by a third man. She didn't know his name, but she wasn't exactly interested in making acquaintances at the moment. "Is this a private party, or are we expecting a few more folks before we have supper on the patio?"

The room answered her with silence.

Blake was okay with that for a moment or two, but when she started hearing her heartbeat thumping through her ears, she felt her skin start to tingle with worry.

"Do you realize how much trouble you caused?"

He actually sounded put out.

"The amount of money it cost to track you, your car, and then all the way to Eagle Rock, Montana. I think I'm going to have to take that out of your salary, Blake. Consider it a fine."

Forcing a smile, she played along. "Okay. That sounds fair."

Seth's eyes were a little too bright in the darkness, but maybe it was just her imagination.

"You know, Blake," he took a step closer, but his gaze was fixed on her face, "I hate to say it but I underestimated you. Looks like you've got a brain in your head. Color me surprised."

Her smiled faded a little, but she was stubborn enough to keep her chin up as she looked him in the eye.

"Imagine my shock when someone from the Public Relations office came by looking for those glasses with the camera built into the frames."

She had to remind herself to be calm. Or at least act like she was.

"And it occurred to me that you were wearing glasses the night you… stumbled into Zoe's cabana where we were *meeting*."

Her mouth went dry in an instant.

Meeting.

How could he say that with a straight face?

How could he talk about it like it was a meeting over coffee and scones at the coffee shop?

"I think you can guess what I'm going to ask you now, Blake." He let the statement die in the coming silence. His eyes watched her closely. And she watched him right back. It was odd to look at him now where she was seeing his 'third' face. The first had been flushed with the pink of rose-colored glasses full of Hollywood magic.

The second had been the cruel face of a man determined to take what he wanted and try to destroy her self-worth in the process.

And this third face wasn't any better, as if he'd finally let any pretense fall away. She got to see the real man under the three-thousand-dollar suit and Armani tie.

The anger she saw in his face wasn't rage or seething

madness, it was calm, cool, and made her whole body start to shiver.

"Where is it?"

She didn't answer. She couldn't seem to get her mind to work as he looked at her.

Seth turned his gaze on Robert and demanded an answer from him.

"I told you," Robert answered him, "she didn't have it on her."

"And you searched her things?"

She had to give Robert a point for not rushing out an answer.

"Broad daylight worked against me. She was staying above a shop. The only ways in and out would be seen by the mechanic who was working there."

"And how do you know it wasn't in the apartment?" Seth's tone was cutting.

"I had a gun pressed to her friend's head and she swore it wasn't there in Eagle Rock."

"She swore? Did you make her cross her heart? Spit shake on it? Oh, I know!" Seth's words spat out like bullets. "Maybe you had her pinky swear that it wasn't in that ridiculous town!"

As much as she hated Robert, she couldn't help but admire how he didn't cower in the face of Seth's anger directed solely at him.

"She told me the disc was here in California. She hid it before she left."

And then she was right back in the devil's crosshairs.

"Is that true, Blake?"

She nodded slowly, trying to keep an awareness of where everyone was in the room. "Yes."

"If you're going to lie, don't. We know it's not in your

apartment. I've already had people go over it with a fine-toothed comb."

"That's why I left," she couldn't keep quiet but there was no use in getting right to the point, and she needed time, "I knew you'd figure it out eventually."

"So, it does exist."

"You know it does." She kept her tone neutral and hopefully her expression followed suit. "I left it here in California. I knew if I took it with me it would be too easy to find me."

He leaned closer and the ghost light made his skin look jaundiced. "Can't say I agree with the haircut, but no one really looks at your hair."

Breathe.

"All you have to do is tell us where it is." He sounded so reasonable, but it had been a long time since she believed him about anything.

"And I will tell you in the morning."

"No!" His shout made her jump and take a half step back. "You will tell me now!"

Cowering before him wasn't an act. She'd never seen him this angry. Cruel? Cold? Sure. But the glint in his eyes truly scared her. The weak illumination of the ghost light gave him a pallor that made her skin grow cold.

"It's someplace that's closed right now."

"We can get in." That from Robert. Strong tone. Over-confident.

"No," she turned to look at him, needing the time, "there's a lot of security. Passcodes. Double locks. The police are always nearby. It's better to wait until the morning. I'll walk in and get it and-"

"We will go and get it." Robert again.

"I hid it, but they won't give you access. I know this sounds crazy, but it's the reason why I hid it there."

"You were expecting us to find you." She couldn't tell if Seth's tone was all ego or a little bit impressed at her. Blake certainly wasn't going to ask. "You put some real thought into this."

Nodding, she met his eyes but kept her expression cool. "I wanted it safe. I wanted Zoe safe."

For the first time, Seth seemed rocked by her words in some way other than anger. His expression was softer than she'd ever seen it.

"She could have had everything you know?" He took a deep breath and let it out. "I was going to give her a big starring role in that new Harlow film. You know, the one about the young girl coming to New York. Zoe," he sighed softly, "was all bright eyes and that sweet smile. A modern-day Mary Tyler Moore. She would have been big with my support. She would have been the next big thing, but then you stepped into it."

His eyes grew cold again.

"I'm not going to let you ruin the rest of my life because you just couldn't keep your nose out of my business."

"I'm not trying to." That was the biggest lie she'd told in a long time. "I know why you want the disc. I'm going to get it in the morning, but you have to wait until then."

Robert stepped in closer. "I can get in anywhere. Just tell me where it is."

Blake brought her hand up to her head and pressed against the throbbing pain in her temple. "I can't tell you where it is. I have to show you and you're not listening to me, Robert. I told you, I picked the place because of the security." She turned around in a tight circle looking at the other men before she turned to look back at Seth and Robert. "I can retrieve the disc in the morning and it's less than eight hours from now. Once you have that I'm leaving Hollywood. Leaving California. I'm going somewhere entirely unrelated to the industry and you'll never have to see me again."

Lying was one thing. Acting like she wasn't going to want to see him with a lethal injection in his arm was quite another.

She could see the wheels turning in his head, the narrowed eyes that fixed on her face.

"I don't know," his shoulders rose and fell on a long sigh, "maybe I like the idea of you close. Time away might make you feel the need to… get chatty. So, first thing's first. You'll bring us the disc in the morning and then I'll decide how far I'm going to let you go."

He turned on his heel and looked at Robert. "Your job, if you think you can do it, is to keep her here and keep things quiet. I'll be back in the morning and we'll get that disc."

She watched Robert bristle under Seth's cold tone and knew that the rest of the night wasn't going to go well for her, but she'd get through it and hope, beyond hope that Adam was coming to bring her home.

CHAPTER 16

THE BURBANK AIRFIELD was close enough for what they needed and when they stepped down onto the tarmac, Adam watched as Hank crossed to two men waiting for them. Both were dressed in black from the neck down, tactical gear.

The three moved back to the base of the stairs as Taz and Tate set up the gear at their feet.

Hank made the introductions. He named off the Brotherhood first and ended that with Adam. Turning back, he gestured to the taller of the two men. "This is Sergeant Thurston-"

"You can call me Palmer," The sergeant saw the odd looks on everyone's face, "or not."

"And this guy is Paxton Fullerton, some of you may have met him before."

Tate was the one to reach across the circle. "Pax, good to see you again."

"Paxton just started with us, but he'll have our backs."

Shrugging, Paxton tilted his head at the sergeant. "*Five* is as good as it gets and he's local LAPD, so he'll help us with access to the studio."

"Is that where they have her?" Adam felt the muscles in his neck tighten up until he was sure they'd snap soon if they didn't get moving.

Lifting the tablet computer in his hand he opened a folder and showed them an aerial shot of the studio with a building marked with a red halo. "We tracked the car that they transported her in and they stopped outside of this building for about twenty minutes before taking the vehicle to the fleet parking lot for Megalodon. There was another vehicle that pulled up. I couldn't get a close enough view to know exactly who it was that entered the building and left about an hour later, but I think we can all guess."

The soldiers nodded around the circle, except for Adam. "Is a guess good enough to bet Blake's life on? Is that all we have to work on?"

Before anyone else answered, Adam's head dropped down until his chin met his chest. "I should have gotten her a phone or given her mine. I should have done something more to protect her. He just walked her out of the diner and put her in a car." The ache in his middle was a black hole, sucking him into the dark cycle of blame. "I failed her."

"Hey," someone clapped a hand on his back, "hey, she's alive."

Adam looked up and saw Paxton standing at his side. "Are you sure?"

Paxton narrowed his eyes at him. "Aren't you?"

Closing his eyes, Adam took a deep breath into his lungs and then let it out. When he was done, he looked up at Paxton and then everyone else in the group, his heart pounding with new life in his chest. "Yeah. I'm sure."

The sergeant gestured toward a restricted gate. "We'll go out that way. I have cars waiting for us to use."

WHILE BLAKE WAITED for the night to come and go, she ignored the pangs of hunger that she felt. She struggled to keep blood flowing into her legs and preserve feeling in her limbs as well. The men took turns walking near the two sets of doors, but after a while they stopped giving her suspicious looks.

The last thing she wanted to give them was trouble.

For her this was a waiting game. And they didn't know it, but she had an extra ace up her sleeve and if things went south, she was going to play it to stall for time.

Seth Coleman didn't know it, but she was going to survive this and get justice for Zoe. Two goals and she was sure she had some decent odds.

And, if that all worked, she was heading to Vegas because it would all be beginners' luck.

Stretching out her legs again, she leaned back against an old wooden crate. Somewhere near the middle of her back there was a splinter sticking into her. Any other day and she would have just moved away from the pain, but as it was, the splinter was keeping her awake and that was good.

Or it would be in the morning.

That's what she kept telling herself.

And that's what she would keep telling herself until she was safe and out of this crazy mess.

THEY MADE their way through a small hole in the back fence. It was small enough that most people wouldn't even know it was there, partially hidden in the shadows of a thick patch of oleander bushes behind a mausoleum at Woodlawn Cemetery.

As they made their way through the narrow space, they had to divest themselves of their gear and put it all back on inside the gate. Once they were all on the inside and redressed, they made their way along the outside of the buildings that made up the patchwork of sound stages in the older part of the studio lot.

And old was exactly what they found. Pieces of sets that looked like they'd been broken off a whole. Rocky outcroppings, the bottom of a Roman column, even the front steps and a door from some kind of fancy home were stacked outside of one of the sound stages.

These unassuming buildings had seen different eras and different countries, wars and romances. If they were there under any other circumstances, their walk might have been more interesting. As it was, those old set pieces were just obstacles and another danger to skirt around.

Hank was at the front of the group and had just made it into the shelter of the shadows of the next row of buildings when he held up his hand for them to stop.

Everyone stopped and found a little corner of the shadows to hunker down in.

It wasn't more than a few seconds before a long, shadow passed between Hank and the rest of the group.

Adam held himself still in the shadows and prepared himself to see who was moving through the quiet backlot. If this person stood between him and Blake, then it really wouldn't matter who they were. An obstacle was just that. Something to move through.

The beam of a flashlight burst through the darkness and swung across the cement, sweeping back and forth, uncovering the wooden braces of a set piece and then the corner of a crate before it glinted off something in the path.

Beside Adam, Taz moved forward, silent as death, readying himself to use his weapon. They'd gone less lethal with their choice of weapons in an agreement with Sergeant Thurston.

Still, their weapons would pack a good enough punch to subdue anyone in their path.

The shadowy figure bent down to pick up the piece of metal on the ground and Hank had the best shot at him, just feet away, but they all waited, wondering who it was.

"Who's there?" The flashlight swung and bathed Hank in its LED halo. "What the hell?"

Everyone tensed as the man stepped into the soft light of the moon and they saw the uniform he was wearing. Studio security.

The man was old enough to carry weight around his middle that made his utility belt sit low on his hips, but that didn't make the gun at his side any less lethal.

"What the hell are you doing here?" The security guard stepped forward and Adam wondered what Hank was waiting for.

Slowly, as if he was moving through chest-deep water, Hank stood and stepped into the light, and Adam felt his breath stick in his lungs.

"Hey!" The Security Guard moved the beam of his flashlight over Hank's body, illuminating his tactical gear from foot to head. "You almost made me piss myself!"

Adam could see Tate look over at Swede with a shrug.

Still, Hank didn't say a word.

Lowering the beam of his flashlight, the aging man let out a belly-jiggling chuckle. "You actors! You're gonna be the death of me someday."

Turning around, he swept his flashlight beam around the area and as the beam passed over each of the men, they followed Hank's lead and stood, lowering the barrels of their weapons but not their awareness of the situation.

"Holy Moly, you guys ain't playing! I've heard of method actors but damn, you boys take this to another level." Turning back to Hank, the security guard shook his head. "I heard they were making some kind of Special Forces movie. I guess you boys are prepping for the role." Nodding, he cast another look over the assembled group. "They're going all out on costumes, I see. Impressive." The security guard set a hand on his belly. "Back in my day I would have put in for that too, but that was a long time ago. Look," he smiled, and shook his head again, "if you're gonna be moving around in the dark, it would be a good idea to call the security office and let them know, because then we would have steered clear of this area."

Hank nodded and the man narrowed his eyes. "Well, looks like you ain't the talkative type, and I get it. You're supposed to be sneaking around all super-secret-like. So, look... I'll head out and continue my rounds. You boys be careful."

A couple of the men returned the guard's wave and the older man started to back away. "Damn, those guns look like the real things."

No one moved until the man had disappeared around the corner of the next building.

BLAKE GREW INCREASINGLY worried when Robert exited the old abandoned office on what would have been the second floor of a normal building instead of a sound stage. He stood on the old catwalk and looked down at her. Pretending she didn't see him leaning precariously against the railing took real effort.

Any attempt to just relax and let time pass was just that, an attempt. She was quickly and quietly losing her sanity.

Worrying had taken over a good part of her mind. Had Annalise really been let go like Robert had promised? Was she home with her baby? What would Adam think about his sister being taken, because of her?

Adam.

If she had stayed put and just accepted the fact that he didn't want her, then this... then she...

No. She had set this whole thing in motion when she left California to go on the run like an idiot.

And trading out her car? What good had that done? If she could believe Robert, the sweet lady who had done her a favor was hurt or worse.

A nagging pain twisted in her gut as she thought about it.

And Sadie. If this ended up hurting her or her family?

Adam. Her thoughts always came back to him. What would he think if Annalise was hurt because of her troubles? She'd never forgive herself.

Never.

A hand closed around her arm and pulled her to her feet.

Turning her head to look, she saw Robert leaning down and searching her face. "What's in that head of yours?"

"M-me?"

"Yeah, you." He narrowed his eyes. "You're planning something."

"No," she shook her head, "I'm just waiting until we can get in to get the disc." She waited for a moment and saw the suspicion in his eyes. "I was just trying to save you from trouble by trying to break into the place tonight. I picked it for a reason."

"Yeah," he smiled, but the expression only left her cold, "you did. And that's why I'm wondering what kind of a trap you're walking us into."

"None!"

He pulled her to her feet, wrenching her shoulder along the way. "Get up."

"Come on," he held her arm tighter as he squeezed it

tighter in his hand, "we are going to have a little talk before he comes back."

This wasn't the plan. The useless thought echoed in her head as Robert moved her toward the stairs. When they reached the bottom, she turned and pushed her back against the railing. "What do you want to know?"

"What are you waiting for?"

Blake shook her head. "I told you. We have to wait until the building opens. Until then I was just waiting. That's what I told Seth."

"Yeah," he tried to move her up the stairs, but she kept a foot planted on the ground, "you said that, but you don't tell Seth everything, do you?"

She felt her teeth grinding together. "What did I lie about?"

"He put you in films and you're trying to bring him down."

"He did the same thing to Zoe that he did to me. If that brings him down then it's his fault, Robert."

"No," Robert's fingers relaxed a little bit on her arm, but she didn't try to pull away, "no, it's your fault."

She heard the slightest dip in the volume of his voice, felt the tremble of his hand around her arm. That's when things shifted for her. Robert was Seth's head of security. The things that he must have seen since Seth created Megalodon, well, it must be staggering. Knowing that she had defied Seth. Seeing how Zoe had left after Seth assaulted her. Blake was absolutely sure that Robert knew that Seth was on his way out.

And he was finally seeing that he was going to be on the way out too. Being the head of security for a man who abused his authority the way Seth did, only had perks when the other man was in charge.

Realizing how close they were to losing it all had to be uncomfortable.

Scary.

And for men used to being in charge, that had to be even more frightening.

That made this even more dangerous for her.

She was the one who could bring them down.

"I'm not trying to hurt anyone, Robert." Her voice sounded tight even to her own ears. "I'm going to give Seth the disc. You won't have to worry about me after that."

"You'll always be there," he nodded, his gaze distant, "somewhere. Waiting to bring us down."

Chills. They raced through her body. "No, Robert. That's not the kind of person I am."

"But you want to get back at Seth for Zoe."

He had her there. "Zoe deserves justice, Robert, but I want to live." That galled her to admit the feelings she was having, but it was true. "I want to have a life beyond all of the crazy of Hollywood. I'm not going to ruin that."

He searched her eyes and she wondered if he would see the fear she was fighting. "How do I know you can be trusted?"

She wanted to argue back. Trust her? She was the one who was being held against her will. "What can I do to convince you? I don't know what to say besides the truth. I want to walk away from this, Robert. I want to go home."

He reached out his other hand and pulled her in close. Shocked to lose the railing at her back, Blake floundered a bit, her feet struggling to find purchase on the stairs. "Just remember one thing, Blake. Whatever you think of me, I've killed before and I'll kill again. If I think for a minute that you're going to turn against me, I'll bury you and I'll never have a single regret about it."

His breath was hot against her cheek and the stench of his cologne turned her stomach into a roiling mess.

"I won't even bother to leave a pretty corpse, Blake. I'll make your body a warning to anyone else who thinks they can screw me over."

"Robert, please-"

The door blew open and bounced off the inner wall with a bang, and before Blake could see who was coming in, Robert was pushing her up the stairs.

She knew that every step up the stairs only heightened the danger so she fought.

ADAM SAW her the instant he moved through the doorway and made a beeline for her across the room. He didn't have time to worry about the other men in the room. Adam had every reason to believe that the other Protectors would handle the pitiful group of security men, and honestly, he would have walked through a hail of gunfire to get to Blake.

Instead, he had to get through one man, and he was spoiling for a fight.

"Let her go!"

The man who turned to look at him was instantly recognizable. They'd all seen pictures of the man at the Bozeman airport and later at the Burbank Airport with his hands on Blake.

They weren't high up on the stairway, but the metal steps had wicked points on them to help people keep traction on the runners. Those metal points would eat up skin like a cheese grater ripped into Parmesan.

"Back off."

The larger man was an easy target, but he had Blake's forearm in his grip. The hold was tight enough to keep her close, but in the darkness, Adam couldn't tell if her fingers looked darker because of the shadows or lack of circulation.

"Adam!" Blake's voice soothed a tiny part of his fear. "He's armed."

As the man shoved her up another step, Adam saw exactly what Blake was taking about. The dark muzzle of a handgun kissed the pale skin of her temple.

He knew then that she wasn't struggling so much as she was just trying to stay upright and alive.

"Give Blake to us," Adam's tone was a hard bark of command. "Surrender her and you'll walk away from this."

"Walk away?"

They moved up another step and try as Adam could to keep his focus, he snuck a glance at Blake and saw her tear-filled eyes looking down at him with open trust.

"That's right," he answered, "I don't want to see you in jail. I don't care about that. I just want Blake back."

"She has to give me the disc. I need the footage on the disc."

"Look around you." Hank's voice came from behind him, but Adam didn't turn. He didn't need to. He could tell by the minute scuffling sounds that the security men were down and bound with zip ties, waiting for whatever fate they were due.

But he also knew that behind him, ready to act, were the other men of the Brotherhood. They were backing his play.

It felt good to have the support.

"You're alone," Hank continued on, "and facing us. That is not a good combination."

"Let. Blake. Go." Adam put his side arm back in its holster and held out his hand. "Let her come to me."

A moment of indecision swam in his eyes. Or was that temptation. Could this man see a possible light at the end of the situation?

Damn, he sure hoped so.

"Let her go and you walk out of here." And right into the police officer covering the door, but he was managing to tell the truth. "Come on."

"Please, Robert." Blake's knuckles were white where she gripped the railing. "Let me go."

Adam latched onto hope when he saw the man's hand ease up on her arm, and Hank offered one more inducement.

"They'll take it into consideration when they bring everyone up on charges."

Blake's eyes widened as her skin lost its healthy color. Adam felt fear knot his insides into a tangled mess of knots as he started for the stairs.

He wasn't sure he was going to be fast enough, but he had to try.

Robert moved with a speed that a big man like him shouldn't possess. Reaching down, he grabbed for Blake's legs and Adam swore he could see the intent on the man's face.

Even from the middle of the staircase, if he tipped Blake over the railing, she'd hit the floor headfirst. Concrete beat bone every time.

Adam had to stop her from going over.

He got his booted foot on the second runner as a start and went from there, his eyes focused on Robert as if staring the man down would help in some way.

By the second step he was done with the stairs entirely. He launched himself into the air, his hands reaching for Robert, determined to pull him away from Blake.

As soon as he made contact with the larger man, he pulled him to the opposite side of the stairs.

They ended up with Robert on his back, Adam with a knee in the other man's stomach and a leg stretched out on the stairs for purchase. The fight went out of the larger man as he stared up into the rafters high above their heads.

"It's over," he mumbled, "over for me."

Adam held the man down on the stairs until someone else came to help him get him onto his feet. He wasn't going to take any chances.

A few moments later, someone stepped over the prone man and took control of his arms, letting Adam get up.

Without another look, he moved over to Blake and found her sitting on the landing, her back against the railing. Her jeans were torn at the knees and her skin had suffered scrapes deep enough that they were weeping blood.

Crouching down beside her, he spoke, but she didn't seem to hear him.

Touching her cheek with his fingers he felt her twitch and start to pull away, but once her gaze found his she reached out for him. He carefully took her by the hands because he could see blood on her forearms as well. He helped her to her feet.

He pressed a tender kiss to her lips, but she didn't let him stop there. Wrapping her arms around his neck she pulled him close and tasted his lips against hers, showing him how much she needed him close.

Adam wouldn't have it any other way.

He gave into her kiss for another moment before he pulled back gently from her body. "We need to get you out of here. I'm going to carry you-"

"No, no..." she put a little more distance between them. "I can walk, I don't want you to hurt yourself."

SHE SAW the look in his eyes and shrugged. "Old habits," she sighed, "but really, Adam. I can walk and I want to."

Looking at the room, at the area surrounding the bottom of the stairs, she felt a weight lift off her shoulders. She didn't have to be afraid of these men. They were the captives now.

Lifting her worried gaze to Adam's, she felt her breath seize in her chest. "Seth. He's not here."

Adam set his hand on her hip and looked over at Hank. "Do they have him?"

Hank spoke into his com and listened to an answer that Blake couldn't hear. A moment later, he nodded at them. "They're bringing him back here."

Blake felt Adam's hand smooth over the base of her spine, easing the tight grip of irrational fear she felt at seeing Seth again.

"You don't have to see him, baby. Not now, not ever again."

Smiling, she touched her hand to the side of his face. "What did I do to deserve you?"

She started down the stairs and Adam followed after her, catching up when she reached the bottom.

Adam gently touched her back again and she knew he was avoiding her elbows. The fabric of her blouse had been torn on the stair runners as well as her skin. To know that he'd noticed and was trying to avoid causing her pain made her love him even more.

"You don't have to see him now," his tone was full of worry, "there will be time later for that. You don't have to be anywhere near him until you're ready."

Stopping just short of the door, she looked up at him and nodded, her eyes brimming with unshed tears. "I know, Adam. I know. But I also know that I want to. I want him to know that I can face him. I want him to know that he lost. And I want him to know that he's going to pay for what he did to Zoe."

She could see him working through the words in his head. Finally, he nodded and gestured to the door.

"And I'll be right here beside you, Blake."

Lifting her hand, she dashed away a tear that slid down onto her cheek. "That means the world to me," she let out a shaking breath, "now, let's get this over with because I don't want to be here any longer than I have to." She sighed. "I know, really brave, huh?"

He brushed his knuckles across her other cheek, the barest glance of skin. "You're so damn brave you humble me, Blake. You kept my sister safe. You don't have to prove a damn thing to me or anyone here."

She heard the others as they agreed with Adam, but her focus was on him. Together they walked to the doors, a little slower than normal because of the damage to her knees. Blake wasn't comfortable leaning on him, but it felt good to have his support.

Outside the old soundstage it was still dark but Blake didn't mind. She felt as if she was stepping into the light for the first time in years. Taking in a deep breath, she didn't have the heavy feeling of Los Angeles smog in her lungs… instead it felt like she was already back in Montana.

When she heard the unmistakable hum of a studio shuttle cart, she looked at Adam. He didn't look concerned so she stood beside him and watched as one of the security guards drove up and stopped just a few feet shy of where she was standing. Two men dressed like Adam got out and 'assisted' Seth out of the back seat. The studio head had his hands bound before him, and a rather lengthy strip of duct tape sealing his mouth closed.

The security officer driving the little vehicle gave her a big smile. "Nice to see you again, Blake."

Confused, but willing to play along, Blake gave the older man a real smile. "Hey, Charlie. What's up?"

"It's been a pretty wild shift. First, I bump into these guys method acting and then they flag me down again for a ride back here." The security guard looked at Adam and the others. "She always remembers me, you know?"

Beside her, Adam smiled. "I bet she does." He tilted his head at the other men who brought Seth closer as he stepped over to the security guard and shook his hand. "Thanks for your help, Charlie. You're a good man."

The security guard chuckled. "Y'all have a safe night, okay?"

As Charlie's cart puttered off, Adam introduced her to the other two men and she was relieved that one of them was from the LAPD. And she was the one who pulled off the duct tape in one quick rip that made Seth howl in pain.

"Bitch!"

Blake couldn't help the smile that touched her lips. "Coming from you, I'll take that compliment."

The color under his skin was a livid red. "Don't think you can bring me down! You're not strong enough!"

Adam was about to reply when she stepped forward, her back ramrod straight. "I'm not going to bring you down, Seth." She saw the flare of triumph in his eyes. "You did that all by yourself. I want you to remember that." She reached out and Adam took her hand without hesitation. "Anything that happens to you now, is because of what you did. The pain you caused. It's all on you." Turning to look at Adam she nodded. "Can we go?"

He pulled her into his arms and kissed her forehead. "Whatever you want, baby."

CHAPTER 17

WHEN THEY ARRIVED at the Autry Western Heritage Museum, Paxton Fullerton and Sergeant Thurston remained at the car, leaving Adam to walk Blake to the front door. They hadn't even made it to the towering glass doors at the entrance when a side door opened and a man gave them a hearty wave and beckoned them forward.

Tugging on Adam's hand, Blake called out to the older man. "Hey, Uncle Joe."

Dressed in his dark denims and a plaid, yoked shirt, complete with pearly buttons, Joe pushed back the cowboy hat on his head and pulled Blake into his embrace. "It's so good to see you, sweetheart!"

"You have no idea how happy I am to see you." She gave him a kiss on each cheek and then stepped inside when he held the door. "I'm not sure if you heard all of the rumors, but-"

"When I heard you'd gone on the run, I have to say I was worried, but I knew you'd be okay in the end."

"You did?" Blake smiled at him. "That was one of us."

He wrapped an arm around her back and gave her a big

squeeze. "Sure did! I knew my girl would figure things out. There ain't no one as sharp as my Sharpshooter Sally!"

Adam laughed as she rolled her eyes. He could tell how much the two cared about each other and they were obviously like family, but he was starting to feel a little left out of the situation.

Joe leaned closer and stage-whispered into Blake's ear. "You gonna introduce me to the young man or am I gonna have to do the honors myself?"

With a playful sigh, Blake held her hand out to him. And Adam took it without a moment's hesitation.

He'd never been a man for public displays of affection, but he took any opportunity to touch Blake in public and most definitely when they were alone.

"Uncle Joe, this is Adam Masterson. He saved my bacon from the pan a few times and he also won my heart, so you two better play nice."

The older man seemed to consider her words.

"Masterson, eh?"

Adam nodded.

"I'm quite the fan of Bat Masterson. Any chance you're related to the great man himself?"

Looking at Blake for help, he was shocked when even she looked at him with confusion. "Bat Masterson was an army scout, gambler and a law man in the old west. A contemporary of Buffalo and Wild Bill, he's one of the enduring legends. And you have no idea."

Shrugging, Adam nodded. "While others were playing Cowboys and Indians, I was playing G.I. Joe." He saw her smile and nodded, conceding, "You did both, didn't you?"

Joe gave Blake an affectionate kiss on her cheek. "My girl is one of them renaissance women!"

"There I agree with you, wholeheartedly." Adam gave her a wink.

While Blake was playfully glaring at him, Joe gave him a straight-forward look. "Well, son. If you've been watching out for my girl like she said, I thank you." He gave a long shoulder lifting sigh. "But I'm not sure about this heart thing. I'll have you know that I'm the firearms expert at this museum and it's not just textbook stuff either.

"I can make a single action pistol sing and I can make a man dance a jig while I pepper the floor under his feet. You understand what I'm getting at?"

He lifted his hand from her shoulder to hold it out to Adam who gave him a good, strong shake.

"I'd lay down my life for her, sir. No questions asked. Anytime, night or day. The fact that she loves me makes me weak in the knees and feel like I'm ten feet tall. I'll take care of her whether she likes it or not."

The older man let out a big guffaw that turned a couple of heads in the gallery.

"You know, I've never understood the idea of being ten feet tall," Joe wondered aloud. "Can't see as how that would be a boon to anyone. Smackin' your head on doorways and trying to find a car, or heck, even a horse to ride would be all kinds of impossible. Woo wee! What a sight that would be!"

The three of them laughed as quietly as they could manage.

"But seriously, girl. I'm so glad to see that you're alive and well. I've been out of the loop as far as the studios go, but after you disappeared, it seemed like everyone had a story.

"What a shame that folks didn't speak up sooner. We might have been able to stop him from hurting all of those women and chasing you all the way to Montana! You'll have to tell me more of that story someday, but I'm sorry you didn't come to me and tell me when he hurt you."

"I am sorry about that, but I was trying to protect you." Blake's features set into a solemn expression. "The way he

196

got away with it was making everyone feel like they were alone. That's the way his secret stayed that way, but I've got proof beyond stories, Uncle Joe. I just need you to let me visit with 'Betsy.'"

The older man gave her a knowing wink and reached for his keys. "She's been lonely without you, honey."

Adam followed behind the two as she went through the gallery and turned into a room with a sign shaped like an oversized 1851 Colt Navy Revolver. The polished brass lettering pronounced it the 'Firearms Room.'

Following behind them, he was only mildly surprised when Uncle Joe opened a display case and reached in for a weapon. Something about Blake opened doors everywhere she went, including his heart.

He was a damn lucky man.

Joe pulled out a rifle and Adam had to smile. It was a beautiful weapon with custom grips.

"That's something special."

The look Blake gave him was filled with pride. "It is, isn't it? They had this custom made for the show and Uncle Joe was the one who took me out to the shooting range and showed me how to use it."

Joe gave her another fatherly look of pride. "It only made sense. If you're gonna hold a weapon you should hold it like you know it. And then they decided it was just going to sit over her fireplace."

Blake grinned. "Still, Joe taught me to shoot it and they put it here in the museum in the television section of the firearms room. They've blocked the barrel so it can't be used to shoot without removing the plug, but the last time I was here I loaded something inside it for safekeeping."

"So that's why you came to see me all rushed and pawin' at the dirt like a filly on the run." Joe gave her a once over. "You could have been a hell of an outlaw in the old west."

Laughing, Blake shook her head. "No thanks. I like the convenience of indoor toilets and air conditioning too much." With an indrawn breath, Blake used her thumb to push down on the piece of metal that would normally have allowed a bullet to be loaded into the rifle. Instead, she held it down and turned the weapon over. Giving it a good shake.

All three of them watched as a little plastic chip fell and tumbled to a stop.

Adam stepped forward and picked up the tiny chip. He turned it over and then back again before looking up into Blake's smiling eyes. "So, this is where you hid it."

Blake handed the rifle back to Joe and gave him a big smacking kiss on his cheek before she looked back at Adam. "I knew if something bad happened to me, Joe would have gone looking in Betsy. He would have found the chip and taken it to the police. I also told Sadie's lawyer the location just in case. He would have showed Joe a video message from me to retrieve the card. Otherwise, I knew it would be safe here. No one touches the firearms room except for Joe."

Holding open his free arm, Adam wrapped his arm around Blake as she stepped in against his side. "You're one smart lady. Seth Coleman certainly didn't understand how wonderful you are."

Joe agreed. "Or how dangerous."

The three laughed at that and Joe returned the weapon to the case, locking it securely with his key.

"You two take your time in here. The museum is at your feet."

Blake shook her head and gave a wistful smile to her old friend. "Maybe next time. Right now, we have to go and give this to the detective outside and then Adam and I are going back to Eagle Rock for a long, long time."

The older man tipped his hat at the two. "Just be happy, honey. That's all I ask."

Blake wrapped her arms around Adam and he cuddled her close.

"I'll make sure of it, sir."

Joe walked away and disappeared around the corner.

BLAKE STOPPED SHORT when they came to the elevators. She gently pulled her arm from his and sat down at one end of a bench. When she looked up at him, she gestured to the other side. He knew she wanted to talk and so did he.

Before he sat down beside her, she was already speaking. "Now that the rush is over, I need to say a few things." She smiled at him, but it didn't reach her eyes. It looked like she was barely able to force the smile onto her lips. "When I left the apartment to go to the diner, that was my fault. I don't expect you to forgive me for putting Annalise in danger."

He ached for her. If she really believed that, he needed to set her straight. "Blake-"

"I did everything I could to make sure she was okay and when you told me that she was safe with Sadie at her ranch, I felt a huge rush of relief, but just because it ended well doesn't mean that everything is okay.

"I left because I was feeling… stupid. I heard you talking to Hank. I heard you tell him that we weren't going to work out. And it's not that I didn't already know that. Everything that happened between us could be explained as adrenaline and hormones and that's fine. I can handle that. I'm not going to be that clingy woman who holds onto a guy that doesn't want to be held on to."

Setting her hands firmly in her lap, she let out a breath. He wanted to speak up but he also didn't want to cut her off.

"I'm not going to be angry or… upset," she continued to speak and he wondered how long her thoughts had been roiling around in her head, "I had a good time. I enjoyed meeting your family and your friends and now that it's all over-"

"And that's where I'm going to stop you."

He saw both hope and fear in her eyes. "You don't have to make me feel better, Adam. You don't need to say-"

"The only thing I need to say, Blake, is the truth. So, if you're done telling me why it's okay that everything ends now. I'm going to tell you why I don't want it to end."

He could see that his words had affected her. He just wasn't sure if she understood what he meant.

"As soon as I said those things to Hank, I felt this crazy twist inside of me. And the words tasted sour on my tongue, because they were a lie. Trouble was, I couldn't figure that out until I said them in the first place.

"And when I figured out that you were gone, that someone had taken you, I knew that I'd been a fool to fight the way I was feeling in the first place."

"No," she shook her head, "what you said made sense. In a short amount of time I not only brought a whole bunch of crazy to you. I put Annalise and Ada in danger and then I dragged you all the way to Los Angeles so you could lead a full-on assault into a movie studio." She shook with laughter and damn it, it felt so good to have her in his arms. "Why aren't you running away from me?"

"Away from you?" He leaned in and claimed her mouth in a kiss. He tilted his head and felt her press tighter against him. A few moments later, he pulled back just enough to see down into her eyes. "Baby, I love you. If you had to go to the ends of the earth tomorrow, I'd follow you there. And then bring you back home."

He felt her melt a little in his arms even when her eyes sparked with some humor. "You know I just might end up staying forever," she bit into her bottom lip while her hands skimmed up his back, "are you ready for that?"

"I'm ready for anything if you're there with me, Blake. You told me once that you knew I'd fix things for you, but you've done that for me too. I wasn't sure I'd ever be ready to have someone... anyone in my life like that, but you're the one I've needed and now I'm not going to give you up... ever."

She leaned in and kissed him. "Let's go," she urged, "Detective Thurston is waiting."

"Let's go."

Taking her hand again, they got up and walked straight through the museum and outside to the waiting detective, dropping the disc into his outstretched hand.

"Thanks, Blake." The detective gave her an approving nod. "You're a quick thinker."

Adam grinned as Blake blushed. "She's brilliant and modest, so I get to give her all the credit."

Paxton held the door open for them to climb in the back of the SUV. "Where to?"

Blake gave his hand a squeeze and she looked out the window on the opposite side of the car. "The hotel, please."

Paxton met Adam's eyes in the rear-view mirror. "I think we can handle that."

Detective Thurston gave his old friend a pointed look. "We? I'm the one driving."

Leaning back in the passenger seat, Paxton crossed his long legs and chuckled. "Take them to the hotel, Thurston, my good man, and step on it."

IT WAS ALL a dream to Blake from there. When they were finally back in their room, Adam couldn't quite keep his hands off her. Blake had been happy to get back some of her clothes. Whatever Seth's crew hadn't ripped or dirtied had been boxed up and returned to her, so the one outfit that she'd managed to get on without dragging fabric over the bandage on her elbow had been her outfit of choice.

And now, she wanted it off.

She'd barely managed to pull it off her good arm when Adam's hands tugged the fabric free of her fingers.

He removed the rest of her clothes, bra, and panties quickly and carefully and she had to admire the speed, ignoring the niggling thought of women he'd practiced on in the past. After all, she was the one standing there, bare and hungry before him, and the look in his eyes said that he was starving too.

When he lifted his hands and pulled his shirt up and over his head her breath caught in her throat. His bare chest, those beautiful muscles, she couldn't resist them. Before his hands could work the button on his jeans loose, she brushed them away.

He covered her hands just as quickly. "Babe," he hissed when her fingertip grazed the bare skin just above the waistband, "I don't want to play right now."

The button slipped free and she bit down into her bottom lip when the cool metal of the zipper pull touched her skin. "Who said I was playing?"

A whisper of sound and his zipper was down. Her hands worked their way free of his and reached around him to slip between his lower back and the denim.

She pressed against him and pushed the denim and his briefs down in the back as she brushed against his front. Blake sighed as the tips of her breasts tightened into hard points using the friction of their bodies. Touching him, having his skin touching her in so many ways, her brain was barely able to function.

All her thoughts were focused on one thing.

Okay, well two.

Bringing her hands around his sides, she pushed his clothes further down, her palms grazing the outsides of his thighs.

"Mmm," she hummed, her eyes closing as she rubbed her body against his, "I love the way you feel."

"You can touch me all you want."

She felt him chuckle through their close contact, but the laughter stopped short when she leaned back and left enough space between them for his jeans to slip all the way down to the floor.

When she leaned into him, she felt the hard line of his cock between their bodies and her breath rushed out of her lungs on a groan.

"If I could get down on my knees…"

Blake heard him groan and felt his forehead touch hers.

"You're trying to kill me, baby." He leaned back to look into her eyes. "And I'd love every minute, but yeah, you're all torn up from those stairs. I think I have an option that would give us both what we want."

"And…" Oh, the dark promise of his voice. It felt like his fingertips were digging into the bottom curve of her ass, or his teeth gently scraping along the column of her throat. "What would that be?"

He lifted his hands and moved them over her body, her bare shoulders, the sensitive curves of her breasts and down to her hips. "Me, inside you. Over and over."

She couldn't help the way her breathing sped up or how each breath made her body move against him. "Yeah, that sounds like a great way to spend the rest of the morning."

Before he could move again, she slipped a hand between their bodies and wrapped her fingers around the base of his cock. "Then again," she slid her hand all the way up until her finger touched the underside of his head and worked her way back down again, "I'm game for staying in all day long."

He nodded and his lips parted as he struggled to breathe.

"Looks like you agree with me." Blake slid her hand back up again and swept the pad of her thumb over the head, smearing his pre-cum over his taut skin. "So, let's-"

His hand closed over hers and squeezed as he swept their joined hands down between their bodies. When she felt the rasp of hair against the back of her hand, they both held still, breathing in the scent of their arousal.

"Get on the bed, baby."

She nodded but didn't move. How could she? Having her hand on him was like standing on the edge of a waterfall, waiting to topple over the edge.

His eyes darkened when he worked her hand free of his cock, bringing it to his mouth, and using his tongue to clean the tip of her finger.

"I feel like I'm always intending to take things slow with you and then a moment later all I want is to bury myself so deep inside you that we don't come up for air until next week."

She smiled at him. "I'm waiting for that to be a bad idea, Adam."

He shook his head at her a moment before he pulled her thumb into his mouth and swept his tongue over the pad of her finger.

"Oh god," her eyes closed and little pricks of light danced in the darkness. "Still waiting," she drew in a breath, "for a bad idea here… because I'm all for everything you're offering."

He drew her hand further away from her and placed a kiss on the inside of her wrist.

Her thighs pressed tightly together and that only made the sensations more than they were, made her hotter, wetter than she had been.

Everything about her was more around Adam.

More confident. More loved.

"I love you, Blake, and if you ever go away again," his eyes shone with the truth of his words, "I'm going with you."

"I don't know why you love me, Adam," she blinked back the tears that threatened to fall, "but I'm so grateful that you do because I'm so head over heels for you I don't know what I'd do if you didn't feel the same way. And right now, you don't have to worry about me going anywhere, but I'm hoping you'll come with me."

She moved toward the bed, drawing him along with her.

"Get up in the middle, baby," he whispered the words into her ear, making her shiver. "Roll onto your good side and I'll show you how this is going to work."

"Not going to argue with that."

Before she'd even settled on the bed, Adam had curled up behind her. His touch was heaven, his mouth made her sigh, and then he was moving against her, inside of her, with her, until they were soaring and falling deeper into each other's lives and hearts.

Blake had never felt that way. She'd never felt so wholly outside of her own skin and full in the center of her soul.

Feeling this way about someone, about Adam, terrified her more than words could say, but as he pulled a pillow up and tucked it gently under her head, then pulled a light blanket over their heated bodies, Blake felt a kind of peace that only he had ever brought into her life.

She might be terrified, but she knew that Adam would be there to help her fix it, because he was the Mechanic.

ABOUT REINA TORRES

Who would have thought that I'd start off as a painfully shy child writing stories and end up as a painfully shy adult writing books and publishing them for others to read? Crazy? That's me!!

When I was a little girl, I read every book I could get my hands on and if I didn't have one available to read, I'd get out my pencils and paper and write down stories and scenes. Waiting for my mom to finish working, I'd duck into the ladies' break room and use the typewriter. I'd feel like Jessica Fletcher, happily tap, tap, tapping away until I got to 'The End.' Couldn't quite get the flourish after that and end up tearing the paper, but it was cool and scary to sit down and read the book or give it to my friends to read.

Now my 'typewriter' doesn't clack the same way and the I don't even have paper to pull out of it with a nod of satisfaction, but I have the joy and excitement of sharing my characters and books with people all around the world!

I hope you'll enjoy reading my books, because I'm going to keep writing as long as the characters are feeling chatty!

amazon.com/author/reinatorresromance

bookbub.com/profile/reina-torres

facebook.com/ReinaTorresRomance

twitter.com/rtorresauthor

Reina writes a variety of romance books from Heat to Sweet and back again…

ALL of Reina's books are available in KINDLE UNLIMITED

Shifter Romance that will bring the Heat

The Orsino Security Series – Three Bears who find their fated mates (BBW)

Her UnBearable Protector

He may be the one hired to protect her, but she brought him to life.

His UnBearable Touch

Her music calmed the beast within him and he brought light into her darkness.

Their UnBearable Destiny

He may be the youngest, but he's no baby bear, and she'll make him earn his place at her side… and love every minute of the chase.

Sylvan City Alphas –

The Tiger's Innocent Bride

When his mate's life is in danger, Devlin has to make the choice between keeping his animal a secret or saving her life. To him there's sonly one choice. Love.

Too Much to Bear

A single dad to a whole house of foster shifters, Boone asks for help from a Dating Agency to find his mate. How could he know that the first try would be the only one he'd need?

The Fighter

When Cage has a hard time understanding how to keep his teenage foster's moods and asks for help. Who knew that the answer to his trouble was also the missing piece of his soul?

Bear His Mark

He's looking for a mate to have and hold and she's afraid she's full of broken pieces. These two opposites might just make the perfect whole.

First Responders & Military Romance with Heat-

Justice for Sloane

When Sloane's life is in danger, FBI Agent Vicente Bravo steps in to make sure she's safe, but his heart isn't safe from falling in love.

Justice for Miranda

Retired Game Warden Miranda finds herself in the crosshairs of a drug smuggler. Her former partner, Trace Carson, is ready to protect her, but is he ready for love?

Rescuing Hi'ilani (Delta Force Hawaii Book 1)

Jackson "Ajax" Guard made a mistake giving up the woman he loved when he joined the Delta Force – Now he has a second chance to love her, but he needs to keep her alive first.

Sweet Western Historical Romance –

Bower, Colorado Series –

Home to Roost

He wasn't looking for love, so he wasn't expecting the perfect woman to stumble across his path.

Imogene's Ingenuity

She came to Bower hoping to work in the print shop and ends up falling for the printer

Three Rivers Express Series –

Always, Ransom (Book 1)

He rode for the Pony Express through a score of dangers on the trail. Danger followed her to her doorstep. Would their love end before it even began?

Always, Wyeth (Book 3)

Tillie lived a life driven by her father's ambition, when she met Wyeth she found joy and love. Will her father allow her to be happy?

Always, Ellis (Book 5)

Ellis spent years in prison for trusting the wrong people, but when he meets the Marshal's daughter he finds himself working harder than ever for redemption... and love

Ellingsford, Montana Series-

Stay With Me

In a world trying to bend their wills, these two lonely souls will find their strength together.

Her Gentle Heart

A man who never asked for help, a woman who gave him what he needed, Her Gentle Heart.

Hold Her Close

A world-weary gambler meets a young woman trying to keep her family together. Is he ready to make a bet on love?

Stand Alone-

The Sailor & The Siren

He found a job on a paddlewheel boat and fell in love with a young woman whose voice and beautiful soul was the melody his heart was searching for.

Sweet Holiday Romance

A Dance for Christmas

His daughter's favorite dance teacher agrees to join them as part of their family on stage in the Nutcracker. What a perfect Christmas miracle to fall in love and make their family real!

Small Town Contemporary Romance with Heat –

St. Raphael, CA Series –

<u>Finding Home</u> (this book also has a SWEET version)

Neither of them wanted to find love when they moved to St. Raphael. Fate & his Nonna had other plans.

<u>Playing With Fire</u>

She swore off 'True Love' – He wants 'Happy Ever After.' How could this end badly?

<u>Healing Hearts</u>

They're both going after their dreams. Little did they know that they'd find love along the way, with each other.

<u>Taking A Chance</u>

They dedicated years of their lives to their careers. When they met, they decided to take a chance on love.

ORIGINAL BROTHERHOOD PROTECTORS
SERIES

BY ELLE JAMES

ABOUT ELLE JAMES

ELLE JAMES also writing as MYLA JACKSON is a *New York Times* and *USA Today* Bestselling author of books including cowboys, intrigues and paranormal adventures that keep her readers on the edges of their seats. With over eighty works in a variety of sub-genres and lengths she has published with Harlequin, Samhain, Ellora's Cave, Kensington, Cleis Press, and Avon. When she's not at her computer, she's traveling, snow skiing, boating, or riding her ATV, dreaming up new stories. Learn more about Elle James at www.ellejames.com

Website | Facebook | Twitter | GoodReads | Newsletter | BookBub | Amazon

Follow Elle!
www.ellejames.com
ellejames@ellejames.com

facebook.com/ellejamesauthor

twitter.com/ElleJamesAuthor